Sir Locke the Gnome

Sir Locke

Books 1 - 6

For all our loved ones who have traveled

to the fantasy worlds of our imagination

ahead of us

Book One

A Case of Cranks and Pranks

a Sir Locke the gnome mystery

A Case of Cranks and Pranks

By Latswin Gilshire, Cleric

Forgive me for taking license with my good friend's stature, but I find it impossible to leave off his title of "Sir." I freely admit that it was a few years after this, his first case, in 842 D.E., that he actually was knighted by the Great Gnome King, Meryur. Lest you misunderstand, to be knighted by the Gnome King is the equivalent of receiving the Key to the city. It's still an honor and I refuse to ignore his title for the benefit of a more accurate historical telling. I offer this explanation because I am sure that my good friend Sir Locke would disapprove of this as he prefers accuracy in all things.

It was the third spring of the second century of the Great Gnome King Meryur's reign. A beautiful Dragost Spring. Sir Locke was in his senior year at the Bardic Académie of Arts and Music, while I was just starting my second year as an apprentice Cleric.

We were to meet at his mother's hubble[1] so we could celebrate his upcoming graduation and the upcoming Spring Equinox. The weekend was before us, not to be wasted!

"Locke, look what they've done!" his mother exclaimed.

She was on her knees in the backyard, tending her garden. She held a small trowel in her hand and she pointed it at her flowers. All of us young Gnomes had a

---

[1] Gnomish: A hubble is a small home

crush on Sir Locke's mother when we were growing up. And she was still what they called a "gnooker[2]."

"Who did what?" I asked.

"Those elk! They ate six of my best flowers."

I shook my head sympathetically. Elk could be such a nuisance to the gardener.

My friend made a cursory examination, most likely to appease his mother and shook his head in commiserate agreement. I smiled at her and waved goodbye, then jogged to catch up to Sir Locke. He had a habit of "walking with a purpose" even if there were none to be found.

When I caught up to him, he decided to quiz me.

"So, how many elk do you think there were?" he asked. We had a nice jaunt ahead of us and I was wary that he might be trying to find a way to have me buy the first round of drinks at the tavern.

I also knew my friend's penchant for mysteries, so I was twice as wary.

"How am I supposed to know the number of elk?"

"Through observation and deduction, my dear Latswin."

I thought I would grow tired of his demonstrations but I have to confess, even after four years, I still found it intriguing.

"Two," I ventured.

"How did you come by that number?" he asked. He couldn't hide his smile. It was a kind, teacher-enjoying-watching-a-student-learn smile. No matter how many times I proved inept at his game of deductive reasoning, he never made me feel stupid.

"Six flowers were eaten, I figured that was too many for one elk, and more than two elk would have eaten

---

[2] Gnomish: A gnooker is a good looking gnome

more. So that meant two elk ate three each." It was all I could do to keep from laughing at my own silliness. I thought I'd get a chuckle from Sir Locke.

"No," he said quite seriously. I looked at him in horror - did he think I was being serious?

And then he smiled and I knew he had bested me at my own game. We both laughed.

We walked on for two more minutes.

"Wait, I know!" I said. He looked at me incredulously.

"Really Latswin?"

"Yes! Zero! There were no elk!" I stopped and waited. This would be the first time I ever got it right. I had high hopes.

"Excellent Latswin. How did you deduce that? What evidence did you spy?"

I gave him a sheepish grin. "None. I figured it out because I know you!"

He seemed to ponder this for a moment and then slapped me on the left shoulder. "Excellent Latswin!"

Two "excellents" in one day!

"I figured it must not have been elk at all. It's the only way you'd know the correct amount of elk. Your mom was wrong - elk did not eat her flowers. Perhaps deer?"

Sir Locke looked disappointed.

"Neither elk nor deer use a knife to cut flowers. And they don't wear shoes."

We continued walking.

"Ok, I can understand you saw footprints, but they could have been yours, or mine, or your mom's."

"Not unless you gained twenty pounds overnight," Sir Locke offered looking pointedly at my slightly rotund figure. "Those impressions are significantly deeper than yours would be, my friend."

"And the knife?"

"Animals don't eat the same length of flower stalk on each flower and they don't make smooth, clean, upward cuts indicating that they are right handed."

"Well you should have been at our dismissal today. You could have probably solved the 'case of the missing parchment,'" I said, trying to change the subject and sounding petulant despite my best efforts not to.

"Was it a deer or an elk that ate them?" he laughed.

"Very funny Locke. The headmaster chided all of us for taking more than the allotted amount. You know how stingy he is in giving out his precious parchment. None of us would pinch it and risk his wrath!"

"I'm sorry my friend. I meant no offense. Perhaps I can look into it when school resumes. I abhor the thought of the guilty running free at the expense of the innocent."

I thought he might be pulling my leg, with his unique form of wit, but I could discern no sarcasm or needling in his tone or face.

"Thank you"

As we entered the tavern a burly young gnome nearly accosted us.

"Vote for change! Vote for Tursdel!" he repeatedly shouted.

Although, perhaps "accosted" was a bit of an exaggeration. I have a reputation for hyperbole, but that's what makes me a good chronicler of Sir Locke's adventures. Well, he doesn't think my stories are that interesting or accurate, but he never stops me from telling them! They've earned us more than one free round of drinks. I sometimes think I should have become the bard and he the cleric.

"He might become the next Town Crier" I remarked.

We took up our normal table in the back. Sir Locke sat with his back to the wall, facing the door as was his habit. I used to think he was paranoid and wanted to ensure no one could come up behind him. I have come to learn that he just wants to be able to watch people. He loves watching people. He said he could learn more from observing people for fifteen minutes than from hours of interrogation.

As it turns out, we arrived at a good time. Drinks were being paid for by the incumbent mayor, Urimop Grarig Aljin Bilgrim Graser. At least that's what his friends called him - his full name being a bit too long for casual hails and farewells. Most just called him "The Mayor," as he had held his post through the last four elections, a pretty good run for the hotly contested position of honor.

It wasn't a surprise that The Mayor was buying the drinks two days before the election, but it was a minor surprise to see him playing waiter.

"Boys, the drinks are on me tonight!"

He plunked down two tankards of ale and slid one in front of each of us.

Sir Locke turned the handle toward him, almost delicately, lifted it and saluted our benefactor.

"I usually charge a little more for my services," Sir Locke said.

"Sir Locke, that's a little…" I wanted to say "rude," but the mayor interrupted me.

"Yes, yes. I know. Do you mind if I sit?" The Mayor asked.

"Of course," Sir Locke said.

"I want to hire you." The Mayor said, pulling out a small pouch and placing it on the table. As if on cue, my friend pulled out his Viol (his musical instrument of choice). It seemed to materialize from thin air. He started tuning it. I decided to sip my free ale and watch. This may be the first time I ever saw my good friend make coin for a performance. While he worked hard at everything, he was graduating at the bottom of his class. His music was ok, his lyrics were a bit melancholy, and his jokes, well, they weren't really funny. His humor was geared toward chemists, theorists, or academics. Unfortunately for Sir Locke, most of those who made up a Bard's audience were not the most elite thinkers.

"No dear boy, I don't mean…" The Mayor began.

"Of course not," Sir Locke said simply, "but let us keep up the pretense, shall we?"

The Mayor nodded.

I nodded also, as not to seem totally dense although I had no idea what was going on.

"So, what mystery do you need solved?" Sir Locke said as he plucked a few notes from the Viol.

"Someone is framing me. The story will come out first thing in the morning, and if I can't discredit the lies, I'm likely to lose the election." He looked like he could use a drink and I thought it was poor foresight for him to have forgotten an ale for himself.

"Did they suggest you pull out of the race?"

"Yes. They said if I pull out of the election, they wouldn't ruin my reputation. That my supposed "infatuation" with the widow Eilissa would be kept quiet. If I didn't, they'd produce evidence of my adulterous thoughts and actions."

"An interesting challenge indeed" Sir Locke said. "I'll take your case." He stood up and went to the bar. He climbed atop a stool and stepped onto the bar. He started playing the Viol, singing loudly.

"It's eleven in the evening boys and girls, it's time to dance,
With spring mid-way through, there's no need to fear.
It's twelve midnight, girls and boys, will you take a chance?
Dragost then Endragost, love's season is here,
It's one in the morning girls, time to go home to bed [pause]
   alone of course, unless you don't care what they'll think!
Not even a kiss? You'll have to tell lies about the girls instead"
It's two in the morning boys, time to close up shop and finish
that drink

The women in the bar giggled. He stopped playing and started his comedy routine. He jumped off the bar, walked over and put his hand on The Mayor's shoulder.

"How do you know if a politician is lying?" He bellowed to the room. Everyone in the bar shouted in unison, "His lips are moving!" and they all laughed, Even The Mayor.

"Remember, the truth will set you free! Don't believe me? Next time your ginny[3] asks if that dress makes her look fat, tell her the truth - 'honey, the dress has nothing to do with it' you say, and see if you're not immediately free of all bonds and ties."

More laughs. I couldn't help but chuckle myself. The crowd got such a kick out of his short performance. So, you may think that he did pretty well, and rightly wonder why I say he was a poor bard. The problem is that he just used all of his material. For most bards that would have been the warm-up, an ice breaker they call it. But for Sir Locke, that was his best (and only) shot.

---

[3] Gnomish: ginny is a girlfriend or wife

Sir Locke sat down again.   He pulled the pouch offered by The Mayor over to himself and without counting it made it disappear into his cloak.

"I'll see you in short order, mayor, I have a lot to do and only an evening to do it."

"Thank you," he said and began to get up.

"One thing…" Sir Locke said, stopping The Mayor's departure. "I'll need access to your study."

"Uh, I suppose that's all right. What time? Now?"

"No, no, in an hour. I have a few errands to run. I'll come around to the side door so as not to disturb your wife."

The Mayor returned to giving out drinks, slapping possible voters on the back, and shaking hands.   I watched for a little bit, trying to imitate my friend's techniques of observation. A few minutes later I gave up and asked Sir Locke the questions that were eating away at me.

"How'd you know he wanted your help, I mean as a detective?"

"Has The Mayor ever bought drinks, hoping to get votes before?"

"Yes, every year…for at least the last four years!"

"Have you ever seen him deliver drinks himself?"

"Well no, but…"

"And my reputation as a detective is already better than my reputation as an entertainer will ever be."

"Come now Locke, you did quite well tonight."

"Thank you, Latswin. Only a good friend can tell such a lie with total honesty."

He lifted his mug, and we did the *clink and drink* thing.

"But how did you know he wanted to keep it a secret? He hadn't said anything about the case yet."

"Why else approach me in the tavern? And why me? If it weren't something he needed to keep quiet he'd have used the constabulary. They work for him after all." I was once again amazed by his mind.

"And about them making him pull out of the race?"

"He said he was being framed - what else would they want on the eve of the election? If they wanted money or a favor, they'd wait until after he was re-elected when they could get more from him. No, the only thing The Mayor has to offer tomorrow would be pulling out of the race."

"So, it's Tursdel, his annual opponent. He's behind this?"

"I try not to jump to conclusions, Latswin. And although it seems that way, knowing who is behind a thing doesn't prove the falsity or truth of it."

We sat for a while sipping the rest of our ale. I wondered why my friend wasn't in a rush. "What can you do when you don't even know what the accusation is based on?"

"We know enough. We know it is based on the supposed adulterous actions of The Mayor toward Widow Eilissa. We know The Mayor is married. We also know that it has to be something that can come out tomorrow. And most importantly, since it's a lie - of that we must assume or The Mayor wouldn't spend good coin, we can deduce that the evidence will be physical, not hearsay."

He finished off his ale.

"It's time to go."

I couldn't help myself. I still had so many questions.

"But why visit in an hour? What do you expect to get done in an hour and what will you learn in his study?"

"So many questions, Latswin! We actually have only 45 minutes left."

As he hurried to the exit he called out "Come Latswin, the gauntlet has been thrown down."

His step quickened as we headed to the constabulary. His normally quick and methodic gait was replaced by an almost hound-dog feverish focus. I did my best to keep up with him.

"Why the constabulary? I thought they didn't know about this?" I asked, hoping to slow him down by engaging him in conversation. I was a bit out of shape.

"No, but they will have valuable information! They almost always do."

My dear friend, who has a very gazelle-like grace about him, and is taller than most of our kind, fairly burst through the door to the constabulary and went up to the receiving desk.

The elderly gnome behind the desk was sitting on a high stool so he could look down (literally, not figuratively) at customers as they pleaded their cases.

"What can I do for you, sapling?"

Sir Locke, being almost an adult, ignored this jab. Instead he countered with one of his own.

"Only your job, kind sir." I definitely enjoyed his humor but most didn't get it. Every word had a double meaning and if you paid attention to the tone and cadence of his delivery, you knew which meaning to infer. I smiled.

Before the officer could finish working out an insult and provide a retort, Sir Locke pounced, winning the round easily.

"Actually, you don't have to even do that. I'll do it for you. Just pass me the log of unsolved cases from today."

The officer hmphed and huraffed. He looked into Sir Locke's face, at his eyes, and saw something there (was it an intensity? A fire?) that made him pause. He spun on his stool and grabbed a pile of parchment. On each was scrolled four or five notes, each with a date and time. He spun back and handed them to Sir Locke.

"Don't worry. I intend to hand them back to you as fast as I can."

I watched as my friend flipped through the pages, scanning them as a hound dog sniffs at the ground, seeking the scent of his prey.

"Aha!"

This shocked me more than anything else as my friend rarely showed emotion. He handed the papers back. The officer had finally come up with a response, pulling together all of his mental resources for the second round.

"Those complaints should be right up your alley. They're just feeble. Dribble of people with nothing better to do than cry about spilt milk."

Sir Locke didn't reply. It could be, in spite of the impressive abilities my friend demonstrated on a consistent basis, that he didn't get the jibe. I thought at first that he was taking pity on the blaggard[4]. The truth turned out to be that he was in one of his super-focused fugues where he blocked out anything but the scent he was following.

"Where to now?" I asked, getting ready for another jog across town if that's what it called for.

"I only want to check on one complaint," he said as we turned down Stone Street. We were headed toward the "bad" part of town. I put my hand on my sword's hilt...you needed to be ready for anything here. Sir Locke didn't hesitate. He stepped up into the House of Seven Sins, a burlesque parlor where you could see the best of

---

[4] Gnomish: A blaggard is a despicable creature

the worst shows in town. He went straight to the bar where the barmaid was leaning seductively over it. I thought she was quite attractive but my friend didn't seem to notice. Instead he climbed onto a bar, for the second time that night.

"Hear now" she half-heartedly said, reprimanding him. He took two long, quick strides, avoiding the beer mugs and bowls of niblets[5] scattered across the bar. He snatched a half-burnt candle from the candelabra overhead. He looked at it, smelled it, turned it once and placed it back, still lit into the holder.

"Thank you," he said to the girl.

"Sure thing, mister," She said sarcastically. "D'ya want to check the dishwater in the back too?"

"Please tell your boss that he was absolutely correct and the culprit will be found out forthwith."

He took two casual steps off the bar, onto a vacant stool, and then back to the floor. I know for a fact that he didn't play sports, but he always had a natural grace and athleticism.

"So where to now?" I asked.

"Latswin, weren't you paying attention? We have only 15 minutes to get back to the mayor's house."

We hustled back to the mayor's house, the largest in the village. It was one of the many perks he would lose if Sir Locke failed to resolve this case.

The Mayor opened the side door, letting us in.

"Mr. H…"

"Locke is fine, Mr. Mayor," my friend said as he slipped into the house. I followed, happy for a chance to sit down. But Sir Locke didn't stop in the sitting room, he went through the doorway on the left straight to the mayor's study. He sat down as if exhausted in the one

---

[5] Gnomish: Niblets are a small snack mix of nuts and nibs

chair for a guest. The Mayor walked around the desk to his chair, having trouble hiding his mix of emotions. He was obviously worried but he was also in a state of excitement. Sir Locke had that effect on people…

"Do you have good news?" he asked nervously. Since there wasn't a chair for me, I leaned against the doorframe. I was still young enough to sit on the floor without discomfort, but I thought it might be a bit too informal.

"If you mean have I proof that you are innocent of that which you are being framed? No." The Mayor's nervous excitement drained out of him and he became dour.

"But don't fret good gnome. You will be exonerated and the culprit exposed. First, I'd like to see your signet ring, official parchment, and your sealing wax."

The Mayor regained a glimmer of hope and happily pulled open the drawer of his desk. He handed Sir Locke the signet ring of the mayor of Little Thoracia, named as such because it was a small replica of the great sea port city to the West. Actually, only the name and the names of two streets matched, but it was good to connect your small town with that of a bigger city. If nothing else it helped with tourist trade.

The Mayor reached into a deeper drawer in his desk and carefully placed a pile of parchment in front of Sir Locke. Finally, he rose and walked over to the book shelf. He hesitated only for a moment before pulling down a large tome. He brought the large book over to Sir Locke, ceremoniously opened it, revealing a hidden compartment cut out of the pages. In it were three blocks of wax. One red, one green, and one white.

Sir Locke stood up, took the book and placed it on the desk. He then took one of the blank parchments and placed it in the center of the desk, and brought the table candelabra closer. Sir Locke carefully examined the signet. He pulled a small dagger from his belt and scraped the raised emblem, collecting pieces of wax onto the parchment. He picked up the shards of wax, pressed them between his fingers and smelled them. They had a red color to them. He then examined the inside of the ring, scraped the inside, producing more residue in a separate pile on the parchment. This he examined the same way. It wasn't red like the other.

"Wax?" I asked as I slid happily into the vacated chair.

"Yes and no," he said. Sir Locke turned to The Mayor, "Who else knows where you keep the official wax?"

"Only my wife."

"How about the Signet? Do you always keep it in the drawer?"

"No, only in the summer. Why?"

"You don't wear it in the summer because it's too tight. The warm weather makes your fingers swell and it doesn't quite fit comfortably." Sir Locke said this more to himself than as a question. "May I examine your hands please?"

The Mayor put them out palms up. Sir Locke turned them over and then back again. "Thank you."

Sir Locke walked over to the window.

"I can save your election and your reputation."

The Mayor almost jumped from his seat with joy. "Really? Are you sure?"

"Very. But first I'd like you to offer the Widow Eilissa a job. Perhaps a position on the town's council? It's not good for a widow to be without a reliable income. It gives people too much to gossip about."

"Of course! I'll do it after the elec…"

"No, I need you to do it before daybreak."

"Ok" The Mayor said, a little confused, but too thankful to argue.

"And I'd like you to invite the Town Crier to join us in the notification. She'll want to do a story on it."

The Mayor just nodded.

"Can you get word to her, the Town Crier? Tonight?"

"Surely I can. She's always snooping around for a story. I'll see to it immediately."

However, he first put the book back on the shelf, put the parchment back in the drawer, and dropped the ring into his vest pocket. Then he went outside the study, closing the door behind him. I could hear him instructing a servant to find Ms. Emogel Strong, the Town Crier, and have her meet us at the widow's an hour before dawn.

"This should be fun," Sir Locke said.

After grabbing a few hours of sleep, my good friend woke me with a consistent tapping on my door. "Let us go and see the results of our labors," he said. I didn't think I had done anything so far, but I enjoyed how Sir Locke always made me feel part of his process. I don't think he actually slept at all, probably too wound up by the excitement of the chase.

We arrived at the widow's hubble at the same time as The Mayor and the Town Crier. Sir Locke seemed quite happy to take a passive role in the proceedings. The Mayor knocked on the door and it was quickly answered by one of the widow's four children.

I understand that you may not be a gnome, so you may not realize that we gnomes are up and about doing chores well before the break of dawn. While it's normal for gnomes to be early risers, it's also normal for gnomes to wait until the sun has risen to make an unannounced visit. Due to this, the widow was quite shocked by the appearance of our party on her doorstep.

"Can I help you?" she asked.

I could see why they would frame The Mayor with wanting to have an affair with the widow. She was a beauty, even at this hour.

"Do you mind if we come inside?" The Mayor asked, bowing deeply.

She smiled and waved us all in.

We all came in and the children seemed to appreciate a break from their daily routine. Chores were forgotten for the time being.

The Mayor was offered a seat in a rocker while the widow and her four children sat on the divan. It obviously played at least two roles - as a couch and as a bed. Sir Locke positioned himself by the front door. I pulled a chair in from the kitchen/dining room and sat upon it, trying to stay awake after our late night. The Town Crier stood behind the mayor with a clutch of parchment, a chip of graphite in her hand, ready for taking notes.

The Mayor blustered on and on about how the widow had been such a good mother and a good wife. How it was time for her to do more for the town, how she was needed on the town's council. There was only one female currently and the town needed her perspective as a woman and a mother. She'd be making enough to afford a bigger house and hired help. Would she please accept? The kids were looking up at their mother in excitement, but before she could answer, Sir Locke interrupted them.

"Excuse me, I believe you have another visitor. Mr. Tursdel has come calling I believe." He flung the door wide open revealing a very rotund, bald headed gnome depositing a dozen flowers tied with a bow and a letter wedged between them. Sir Locke stepped in front of the doorway, blocking the room from his view.

"Ah, ah." He seemed frozen to the spot.

"Can I help you?" Sir Locke asked with authority, as if he had lived there his whole life.

"Ah. ah. Well, I was just dropping this off for...for The Mayor." The items were still in his hand.

"Why isn't he dropping it off himself?" Sir Locke asked.

"Well...ah, he's shy."

"The Mayor?" Sir Locke asked with true amazement in his voice. Everyone in the room was quiet, enjoying this much more than any theater they had seen in recent memory. The oldest girl looked at The Mayor and giggled. He smiled at her and put his finger to his lips.

"I mean, well, he *is* married," Trusdel said in a loud whisper. He was finally regaining his balance.

"So, The Mayor asked you to deliver this to the widow Eilissa? How long ago did he charge you with this task?"

"Only moments ago. He's standing over there, across the street. Behind the Potter's door post." He pointed and then waved as if expecting a wave from the shadows in return.

"Well I doubt that. Why don't you call him?" When Sir Locke was like this, his demeanor didn't really allow an argument. The poor fool didn't even think to ask who Sir Locke was or why he was there. He was trapped in his own deceit and was doing his best to grasp at any straws he could find."

"I   told   you,   he's   a   married   man." "I'll do it for you. Sir Locke took a step forward, and shouted, "Mayor Urimop Grarig Aljin Bilgrim Graser, come on out!"

The man turned, still playing out his farce, looking toward the shadows as if he expected The Mayor to come out into the street at any moment.

"I told you he wouldn't..." he started as he turned back to Sir Locke. He stopped speaking when he saw The Mayor standing in the doorway beside my friend.

The Mayor picked up the flowers and pulled the letter from the bouquet. The folded note was sealed with the unmistakable image of the mayor's signet ring. He broke the seal and held the letter up so he could see it using the light from behind him in the house.

"Not bad. Not good, but not bad. Your prose is very juvenile, but the handwriting is quite close to my own." The Mayor said.

Tursdel dropped all pretense at this point.

"It doesn't matter! A rumor is as good as the truth, and a rumor with props is better. Your being here just ensures success! It's your word against mine! And everyone heard your young friend here yell for you! They'll believe my version when they see us all standing here!"

He backed off the porch and gave a shout, "Come on everyone - look who I just caught..." before he could finish digging a full-sized grave for his political aspirations, the Town Crier elbowed her way past Sir Locke and The Mayor, feverishly making notes.

"Wow. This is the best story I've had to share in years! Thanks, Tursdel. You are now officially my favorite politician ever!"

Doors across the street opened. Doors to the left and right opened. The widow's neighbors came out to see what the ruckus was all about. As fast as he could, which was not that fast, Tursdel ran. Word was that he kept running out of town and hasn't been back since.

I was tempted to end the story here, you know, "all that ends well."

But I assume you, like me, wanted to know how Sir Locke did it. On the way home that morning I asked my friend. Now, this is when I understood why he was trying to become a bard. The joy in his eyes while regaling me with his reasoning skills was only surpassed by the excitement on his face when he was in the heat of the chase.

"My dear Latswin. I have tried before, but it seems that this school of reasoning is beyond you. And while you have a keen eye and mind for healing, I dare say you are one of the most unobservant gnomes I have had the pleasure of knowing."

"That's because I'm the only one who likes you!" I said joking and I was glad he smiled. I was worried I had said in jest something too close to the truth.

"In reality Latswin, it's that you're the only gnome, besides my mother, that I truly like." He said this with more seriousness than I could deal with. I was turning his triumph into a sad introspection.

"Enough about me. How'd you do it?" I said changing the subject back to the original topic.

"Ah. But weren't you along for the ride? Everything was there to see. Well, except the last proof." He went through each in chronological order for me.

"My mother's flowers, six of her best, cut, not eaten. Most everyone knows if you want store-bought quality flowers, without buying them, my mother's are the best."

"Yes, but Mrs. Eorwyn's are a very close second!"

"Right you are!"

"So why not steal hers?" I offered, not entirely sure why any flowers should have been stolen at all.

"Oh, he did. She had six stolen from her garden also. Twelve from one garden would be too obvious."

"But why not just buy them?"

"It's hard to claim that they came from The Mayor if you were seen buying them."

"Ah!" I said realizing the problem of witnesses.

"Ok, but what was all that about dancing on the bar? And how did you know Mrs. Eorwyn had flowers stolen?"

"All will be made clear shortly, my dear Latswin."

After a dramatic pause, a common ploy among bards, Sir Locke continued.

"Remember, the culprit had already told us, through the threat on The Mayor's reputation, that he planned on incriminating him with the widow. With the election only days away, the motive was obvious - someone wanted The Mayor to lose."

"So, I was right all along. I said it was Tursdel!"

"Yes, you did. But that wasn't deductive reasoning, that was guessing. I didn't know for sure until I caught him delivering the contrived evidence himself."

"Because you caught him in the act." I declared.

"No. Do you want to know how I did it or do you want to keep guessing?"

"I'm sorry. Please, continue." I said, feigning hurt feelings. Sir Locke was not moved by my acting and ignored my pout.

"So, with the need for haste, the culprit would not have time to waste. He needed something that could only be from The Mayor."

"The signet!"

Sir Locke stopped walking and turned to face me, irritated.

I smiled. "Sorry."

"Yes, the signet. But while the ring was easily accessible in the top drawer of the desk, the wax was well hidden. And our culprit wanted red wax, to signify love. The burlesque house has red candles."

"He needed a pen and ink, he wouldn't have the time to do it sitting at the mayor's desk. Whenever he broke in, he would want to get out quickly, forge the love letter, and then return the ring. A wet quill or a spill of ink would alert The Mayor. He stole the ink from the calligrapher Svenkil, the quill from Yohansen's peacock, and the parchment from your school."

"But how do you know all of that? We didn't go to the calligrapher's, or the school, or speak to Mrs. Yohansen!"

"Where did we go?"

"Only the constabulary."

"And…"

"And you looked at the log of unsolved crimes."

"Yes, actually I only looked at the log of the 'cranks and pranks' - what they call the cases too small or trivial to investigate. They jot them all down to make the 'cranks' who are complaining feel that the 'pranks,' which have been perpetrated against them, will be looked into. You know how much we gnomes like to keep track of everything we own...even down to the last feather. They were all there. The flowers from Mrs. Eorwyn, one missing peacock feather, and an ink well mysteriously only half full when the calligrapher was sure he had filled it just the day before."

"There was an official decree making the sixth Sunday of summer, the week before the Summer Solstice at the

end of Frogost[6], a day of celebration in honor of the
Gnome King's birthday. It was handwritten by The
Mayor. It was missing from the town hall's bulletin
board, and later returned."

"And the Burlesque owner was sure that he had
replaced all the candles at the same time, so he wanted to
know who had burned down one of his candles faster
than the others."

We turned a corner and I could see his hubble ahead,
his mom back to gardening even at this early hour.

"I wanted to examine the candle, and as I surmised, it
showed that it had not only been burned more than the
others, but it had been turned as to drip wax from it. It
has a nice perfumed scent used by the proprietor to
enhance the aroma in the establishment."

I must have looked incredulous.

"The owner is quite the entrepreneur. You don't
have to have a fancy place to be classy."

I nodded, realizing that I had been a bit of a snob.

"The parchment you mentioned yourself when we
met."

"Why so much ink, paper, and candle? It was only
one love letter, right? Or did he fabricate more?"

"No, just one I venture. If he had time to hire a
Kenku[7] (they are excellent forgers), it could have been
done in one or perhaps two tries. But he had to forge the
mayor's handwriting himself. It needed to be good
enough to pass a quick scrutiny. It's why he needed the
decree from the town hall."

"Ok, but how were you sure?"

"The ring."

---

[6] Frogost is the summer season in Aethrofell
[7] Kenku is a bird-like humanoid creature

"Ah, the wax. I saw you smell it. It was the same wax as the candle, right?"

"Yes. It was."

"So that was it? That was enough, right?"

"No. All of those petty thefts and the wax could have been done by The Mayor so he wouldn't be found out. The same reasons our culprit needed to take rather than pay, avoid witnesses, and do everything in secret would have also fit the modus operandi of a man trying to hide an adulterous desire from his wife. That's what made Tursdel's plan so beautiful."

"Alright then how did you know it wasn't The Mayor? Because he hired you?"

"He hired 'us,' Latswin," he said, patting me on the shoulder and then gripping it with affection. "No, many guilty people try to look innocent by claiming to want the truth. No, I knew it by The Mayor's hands, and then confirmed it with Tursdel's. The ring was tight, too tight for The Mayor to wear during the summer. So, he left it in the drawer. I found bits of skin and a hair from a knuckle on the inside of the ring."

"That's why you looked at the mayor's hands!"

"Yes, and later when Tursdel was pointing, I noticed a raw knuckle on his right hand. He didn't need to put it on to seal the wax, but he couldn't resist. He wanted to be mayor pretty badly. Unfortunately, he, like The Mayor, has big hands and he couldn't get it off. He ended up yanking it off and scraping his knuckle in the bargain."

"Amazing Locke!"

"Actually, it was elementary, Latswin, but thank you for the compliment."

The End

Book Two

The Death of a Champion

a Sir Locke the gnome mystery

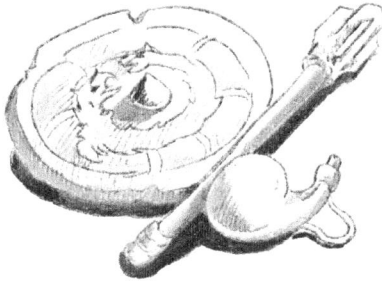

The Death of a Champion

By Latswin Gilshire, Cleric

I feel it prudent to offer a disclaimer for this account of what turned out to be a very stressful case (for me). It took place at the Autumn Gladiatorial Games in Grimstone[8]. I was always a big fan of the games and was excited to finally attend one. My depiction of the games within are not as brutal and bloody as the games actually are. The level of violence was much higher than I had imagined and I confess that I've lost much of my enthusiasm for the games. So, in an attempt to make this more readable for a wider audience, I have taken some liberties. Please forgive me for any inaccuracies within.

And yes, again, I am taking the liberty of using his title although he actually hadn't been knighted yet. In my defense, he was knighted on the way home from this trip, and this case was a major factor in his being awarded the honor.

It was early in the first summer of the second century of the Great Gnome King Meryur's reign. Sir Locke had just graduated, while I was in my second year as an acolyte. I hadn't decided on my specialty yet, although my friend's exploits (and my inclusion in them) had me

---

[8] Grimstone is the capitol of Aethrofell

seriously thinking about studying how the body works. It wouldn't be as lucrative a field as others, but it would make me more useful to my friend in his investigations.

This particular case occurred at the beginning of my friend's career as a detective (and as a bard). In truth, it was only his second actual case. He had not yet picked a bardic college to continue his studies, instead seeking a rumored "School of the Detective."

As a belated graduation gift, my father's brother's uncle, Gobnac Tadyddwiem Densnag Gilshire, sent me two tickets to the upcoming Autumn Gladiatorial games in Grimstone. They were seats in his luxury box, some of the best seats in the stadium. This was quite fortuitous, since I had yet to find a gift for my friend's graduation.

The trip to Grimstone, the capital city of the Empire, was an adventure in and of itself, but one that I will not chronicle here. It would be more a bawdy tale of youthful carousing, than one detailing the most tragic mystery I think Sir Locke will ever solve. The capital's name comes from the bluffs overlooking the ocean which appear to form a screaming, skeletal face…"Grim Stone." The city is the largest and most powerful city in the empire, the seat of power, and the meeting place of the High Council. But the reason the city is a destination for thousands each year, is because of the Great Gladiatorial Games. Twice each year, people travel from across the Empire to witness the major events; the spring and autumn games.

We arrived two days before the games began. This gave us time to visit with my relative, a bit of a renowned character in the city. He seemed to have no discernible means of income, but lived lavishly. I tried to engage my friend in solving this mystery, but he was uninterested. We toured the city (it was our first time in the capital) and enjoyed my relative's hospitality. It wasn't until the opening bout of the games that my friend found something that made the trip memorable.

The Autumn Games opened with an impressive procession of gladiators, nobles, and beasts. They paraded through the streets to trumpet blasts and criers making announcements. The first day was to be full of pomp and circumstance. On our way in, my friend took note of the bookies collecting bets, it seemed gambling on the games was big business.

"Interesting…" was all Sir Locke would say but he stood watching a transaction for, what seemed to me, a long time. I'll admit, I wanted to get to our seats to enjoy the spectacle. We had tickets for Gobnac's luxury box which was near the field. This was optimal since gnomes are one of the shorter races (we are easily mistaken for human children) and we didn't want anyone blocking our view.

As it goes, we would see very little of the games that Fall.

The opening bout was promoted as the retirement swan song for one of the Games' greatest champions, Tyann Rit the barbarian vs. the new rising star, Kaiden "The Killer" Cooper.

It was then, and I am ashamed to admit, only then, that I realized my friend was on this trip totally for my benefit. He had shown his customary understated excitement upon receipt of my gift (which was admittedly a re-gift), so I was not taken aback. And on the journey, he seemed to enjoy himself, although now when I look back I realize he spent most of the time writing and drawing in his travel log. Later I learned that he was making notes on the different folk we met. Height, weight, shoe sizes. Hair, eye, and skin colors. Distinct features and mannerisms. And now, seated close enough to be possibly splattered with blood, he was busy looking about the crowd instead of the arena. He had his pad and charcoal at the ready. He barely paid any attention to the announcer's build up to the first match of the day.

"Locke, don't you want to watch the match?"

"Latswin, my dear fellow, you do know it's all fake, don't you?"

I wasn't sure I heard my friend correctly as at that moment the challenger, The Killer entered the arena. His name had an ominous sound to it, but he had never killed anyone in the ring. Reportedly he was an ex-general in the army of the Dragon Empire and had killed various enemies in battle. A decorated war hero. Sir Locke said this was unlikely and that Kaiden's entire backstory was probably pure fiction.

"The Killer's" entry into the ring was met with a rising chorus of boos.

It was clear who the crowd favorite would be for this match.

The champion was announced next. This was his eighth (and final) Gladiatorial Game. He had started, as most do, in the smaller games that went on monthly, but his unique style and flair quickly gave him a spotlight in the Spring Games, four years ago. He beat the reigning champion, a Goliath named Agnar, and held the spot ever since. He was known for dressing in only a fur-lined loincloth. He fought with a mace and a shield. No armor, no helmet. His long hair flowed around his massive shoulders as he'd fly into one of his famous rages, bull-rushing a foe.

But his most endearing trait, the reason the crowds loved him, was he was always fair. If he disarmed his opponent, he'd hand them back their weapon. If they were down, he waited until they got back up. He never hit an opponent who wasn't looking although his opponents regularly tried to attack him when he wasn't ready.

Sometimes the champion was a "villain," and sometimes he was a "hero." Tyann was a hero.

Tyann Rit, simply called "The Champ," entered the ring to an ever-rising crescendo of applause. He came running into the ring, hair wildly flying about his face. More cheers and now girlish screams. He stopped and scanned the crowd. Then, as if he found the person he was looking for in the audience, pointed into the stands. Cheers rang out louder. He then pointed to another, and then another. More screams of joy and cheers met his every move.

I almost felt sorry for Kaiden. He waited, twirling his sword, for the signal to start.

Tyann grabbed the wineskin tethered to his side, lifted it high over his face and with one hand squeezed. The stream of liquid expertly flowed into his mouth. He gulped down a few swallows and then directed it into his face. He let the pouch fall to his side and vigorously shook his head like a dog coming in from the rain. The crowd went crazy. They knew his every antic and loved every minute of it.

Finally, the announcer made the proclamation, "Let the battle begin!"

Death was an irregular occurrence in the Gladiatorial Games. Most deaths occurred when the match pitted monster vs. monster, or hero vs. monster. These were gorier spectacles for the low-brow audience (they screamed for blood).

As the two massive combatants started circling each other, the crowd started chanting Tyann's name. I was mesmerized by the show. I stole a peek at my friend and at least he *seemed* to be watching.

The rest of the box was as captivated as I, except our host, Gobnac. He seemed as calm as Locke.

Tyann gave his famous shout as he charged forward. He took a wide sweeping swing with his mace, at the head of his foe. At this Locke leaned forward but instead of the wide-eyed excitement I knew was on my face, he was studying the battle with his keen ferocity of focus. Kaiden easily ducked beneath the blow, stepped in, and swung with his sword. Tyann blocked this expertly, slapping it away so that the flat of the sword hit the metal on his shield making a loud clang that could be heard outside the stadium. Unfortunately for Tyann, when he blocked the strike, it left an opening for Kaiden to follow with an elbow to Tyann's jaw.

"Impressive," Sir Locke said with a wry smile.

Tyann must have been hit extremely hard as he was lifted off his feet and landed hard on the ground. Kaiden, instead of trying to finish off Tyann, turned to the crowd and started exhorting them for cheers. He received only boos. He continued to walk around the fallen champion, raising his arms repeatedly.

Tyann didn't move.

Finally, after what seemed like minutes, Kaiden turned back to the fallen champion, his shield at the ready, his sword out in a defensive posture.

But still Tyann didn't move.

A second later, Tyann Rit's manager came running from the pit. He slid to a stop next to the still body of his fighter. He put his ear to his chest. He opened his eyes.

He gestured wildly back to the pit and four men came running out, two carrying a stretcher.

Kaiden was confused. Instead of raising his arms in triumph he walked, as if dazed, over to Tyann. He dropped to a knee beside him and seemed to be distraught. It took another five minutes to clear the field for the next match.

"What happened?" I asked Gobnac.

"It looks as if I just made a ton of gold," he answered.

"You bet against the champion?" I asked.

"Yes, I did. You could say I had a hunch."

I looked at my friend to see what he would have to say, but he was packing up his notebook and charcoal.

"Where are you going? The games have just begun" I said.

"Yes, but we may have more important things to do."

"Why do you say…" and before I could finish, I heard the announcement.

"Any clerics in the house? Please report to gate 9." This was repeated three times before Sir Locke nudged me from my stupor.

"That would be you, old friend." He pulled me up by the elbow and we headed to gate 9.

When we made it to the gate it took a while for us to convince the guard that we were not some lost children (the lighting was not very good) and that I was a cleric answering the call. I think it was my beard that finally convinced him. We were taken into the tunnels.

"Wouldn't they have clerics on hand?" I asked my friend.

"Yes, they would. Perhaps they are looking for a specific type of cleric?" Sir Locke said.

When we reached the champion's dressing room, his manager was interviewing a cleric and there was one waiting. Each was turned away. Then it was our turn.

"I am a cleric," I said as I stepped forward.

"Do you have any training in detecting cause of death?" the manager asked.

"Well, I don't…" I began to explain that I was still in school and while it was an area of study I was contemplating, I had not yet gained any useful training. But Sir Locke interrupted.

"Yes, he does. Where is the body?"

"In here. We need to determine if he was poisoned and if so, how. The magistrate is on his way." He opened the door and ushered us in.

The manager closed the door, staying outside. We were alone inside the dressing room with the body of the great Tyann Rit, champion of 8 straight Gladiator Games, lying on a table.

"How did you know he was dead?" I asked.

"It was the only logical reason to need a cleric with different skills than they would have on call. I'm sure the ones working the games can heal, mend, and probably even revivify. But, Latswin, I don't actually know that he is dead. Perhaps you should check."

I checked for signs of life.

"He's gone, nothing to be done," I said.

"There's a lot to be done," he said and I remembered why they called for us.

"How am I to determine the cause of death? I know nothing of poisons or forensics," I said.

"My dear friend, please don't be offended, but you know a lot more than you realize."

I looked at him, confused.

"And what you don't know, he will tell us," he said, pointing to the dead champion. "There's a lot that can be learned from the dead."

Understanding dawned on me.

"Yes, I think I see what you mean." I carefully began an examination of the body, from head to toe, looking for any cuts or bruises. Luckily no one was in the room with us as they may have wondered why a cleric was stripping the patient. Then again, it would have been helpful to have more hands for the task as even removing the scant clothing Tyann wore was not easy. He must have weighed nearly 300 pounds and his hand was bigger than my head.

I continued my examination, looking for anything and everything since I had no idea what exactly I was looking for. Sir Locke joined me, directed me to look at his fingers and knuckles. He pulled his dagger and scraped under Rit's fingernails. He opened his mouth and examined his teeth. He then did an odd thing; he smelled the champion's breath. Since he was dead, he had me push down on his diaphragm to force any air out of his lungs. I caught a whiff. There was no odor I could smell, outside of the normal healing potion likely given to him by the first cleric on the scene.

Finally, he removed the silver coins from his eyes, and pulled his lids open.

When we had ensured he had his clothes (what little there were) back on properly, we called in his manager.

Carter Vaughan had been Tyann Rit's manager since he first became a gladiator. It was a good relationship by all accounts, both gaining in fame and making a nice living.

"What happened? He was in great health. Was he poisoned?" Carter asked as he entered the room.

Behind him, holding each other for comfort, were Tyann's wife and daughter. Both were in tears. Finally, after them came the magistrate (someone our size) with two guards towering beside him.

"Obviously there was foul play!" the magistrate, a self-important halfling, announced. At this the women wailed louder and in unison rushed to the body of Tyann. They wrapped themselves around and over him as if to protect him from any more harm. I thought their tears were very real.

"Obviously? To what extraordinary talents in observation can I attribute this deduction?" Sir Locke said sternly. He reminded me of one of my teachers at university.

"Hmph. Well. Champions don't just drop dead from a single blow!" He looked up at his guards and their nodding heads gave him some confidence. "Am I wrong?"

"So, you have surmised that there was foul play simply due to the observation that he died?" Sir Locke actually looked interested.

"There was a lot of coin wagered on this bout. There was bound to be something amiss. We thought there might be a fix on, you know, one of them throwing the fight. But if you are sure he's dead, then we're changing the charges to murder."

"I'm sure he's dead," I said.

"Then murder it is." The magistrate said this as if he were the stadium announcer.

"And who have you deduced carried out this nefarious deed?" Sir Locke asked. I wasn't sure, but he seemed to be interrogating the magistrate.

"Gobnac Gilshire!" He almost shouted it as if in front of a jury. He actually lifted his finger in a triumphant exclamation.

"Because…" Sir Locke spoke so calmly, so softly compared to the blustering of the pompous fool of a magistrate that I almost didn't hear him. My ears were still ringing with my family's name.

"He wagered ten times more than anyone else for the champ to lose. He had the most to gain. Ipso Facto, guilty!" He said this last phrase like a wizard making an incantation.

"When is the trial?" Sir Locke was still calm. He didn't seem surprised or upset, while I on the other hand started toward the magistrate, my fists reflexively clenched. Luckily for all those involved (especially me), Sir Locke put a restraining hand on my shoulder and whispered to me, "Not yet, my friend. Not yet."

"Trial?" he actually laughed. "The execution will be the kickoff event for tomorrow's games!" At this he turned and left with his two guards.

"What a fool! I have to see Gobnac…" I began, meaning to find my relative no matter the obstacles.

Once again, my good friend held me in check. He grabbed my shoulder more forcefully.

"I'm sorry Latswin, but we have a lot of work to do and very little time to do it."

This time I understood. My relative would be executed first thing tomorrow if my good friend couldn't prove him innocent. And from what I had seen, there wasn't any evidence to help. He turned to the manager as he instructed me to stay with the two moaning women.

"Mr. Vaughan, can I trouble you for a word or two?"

"Well, yes. But you still haven't told me why he died? Was he poisoned?"

"Let's speak in private," Sir Locke suggested.

They exited the room. The women were incoherent the whole time they were gone. After what seemed to be an interminable amount of time, Sir Locke returned, without the manager. Two others came in with him. They were dressed in long black robes, with black hoods. They were the morticians. They'd prepare the body for whatever ceremony his wife wanted. As they spoke with the widow, Sir Locke pulled me aside.

"I need to speak with the two of them."

I nodded.

"Separately."

I nodded again. If you know me, and from reading these accounts of my friend, you may have gained some insight, you'd know that I have not the quickest mind for riddles. I can't keep up with my friend on my best, and his worst, day. But that day, in that moment, I didn't feel I had to. I didn't want to ask any of my normal questions. I had no curiosity on why or how he was going to solve this case...just that he did so quickly. I had a single mindset...I was going to do whatever my friend asked me to do, and do it well.

I walked over to the daughter and helped extricate her from her father's body. I gently escorted her to my friend. "I'll stay with Madam Rit."

He nodded and escorted the young woman out of the room.

I watched as the mother first discussed, then bickered, and finally bartered with the two morticians. Finally coming to an agreement on the plans for the body, they left the room. She didn't seem to notice her daughter's absence. She went over to the body and much more calmly laid a hand on his chest. With her other hand she brushed his hair with her fingers. She was speaking to him in a low voice.

I felt bad listening in, but I knew my friend would want to know everything about everything so I listened.

After a while my friend came back, again alone. I only thought this strange for a moment before I refocused to be ready if Sir Locke needed anything.

He approached the widow, put an uncharacteristically compassionate hand on her waist and pulled her to him. He wasn't normally good with people or displaying emotions. His bardic training in acting seemed to be paying off.

"There, there."

She allowed him to pull her into a fatherly embrace. She sobbed on his shoulder (he was a good foot and six inches shorter than her). When she seemed to be over her crying, he broke the embrace and offered her a handkerchief. I have no idea where he got it, since he never carried one that I knew of.

"Were you afraid?" he asked. I knew this was the beginning of the interrogation, but it again seemed very uncharacteristic of my friend. It seemed off topic and too gentle.

"Afraid?" She looked back at her husband's body. "Yes, I guess I was."

Sir Locke waited patiently.

"He should have retired last year. He was so stubborn!"

"Was he in good health?" I again wondered at this line of questioning as it was obvious that Tyann Rit was in great shape.

"Yes, yes…"

"But?" he prodded.

"He was old, older. All of the challengers are young, really young compared to him. He didn't need to go out with a big show. He could have retired quietly and, and…"

"Everyone loved him," Sir Locke added.

She turned from Sir Locke and once again embraced her husband.

"You old goat, why'd you have to have one last show?"

We left her like that. I didn't see that he got anything from his questions, but he seemed satisfied.

"Now can I see Gobnac?"

"Yes, of course. I have a few questions he can help with."

We went to the makeshift holding cell, halfway around the arena. It was a large cage used for some of the beasts used in the games. It smelled of dung and blood. Gobnac was chatting with the guards, seemingly relaxed.

"Can we have a moment alone with the accused?" Sir Locke asked the more decorated of the two guards. These were not the stooges that accompanied the magistrate, but they wore his colors.

"Not allowed," he said.

"No worries then," Sir Locke said with a small smile. Unusual I thought.

"Gobnac! We will…" I began, but Sir Locke cut me off. At least *this* was usual.

"I'm sorry, we don't have much time. I need information."

"Of course. I'm not sure what…"

"Just answer three questions, as honestly as you can," he glanced toward the guard as he said this.

"We found traces of a red liquid that smelled of Death Lily in and around Rit's mouth. If you wanted to buy a poison, enough to fell a large man, where would you go? Discreetly, of course." Sir Locke jotted down the address of an apothecary.

"Who did you lay your bet with?" More note taking.

"How well can you fight? Say with a sword and shield?" Hesitation. Then he smiled at Sir Locke, a mischievous, conspirator's smile. "Yes, I thought so. Great. Go ahead Latswin, but we only have moments to spare."

I spent the five minutes allotted to me assuring my relative that Sir Locke would solve this mystery and exonerate him. He listened earnestly, nodding when appropriate. He seemed to be considering everything I said carefully.

Sir Locke, during this time, was making more marks in his book.

"That's enough time, let's go." Sir Locke closed his notebook.

"Enough time for what?"

"For a fair head start."

I had forgotten my decision not to ask questions.

I gave Gobnac one more reassuring smile, and hurriedly joined Sir Locke. My relative's life was in the hands of my friend, a young bard who would rather solve riddles than entertain an audience. I hoped he was up to the task.

"Where to?" I asked catching up. He was definitely in his zone.

"We have to get to the apothecary before he leaves."

"Who leaves? What apothecary?" I mentally groaned. I couldn't stop myself from asking questions!

"Weren't you paying attention Latswin? How many guards were there, watching one caged gnome?"

"Two. I hadn't seen them before but they work for that fool." I thought I did pretty well and was trying to show my friend that my powers of observation were getting better.

"How many were there when we left?" I couldn't answer. I hadn't paid any attention after I started talking to Gobnac.

"One of our attentive guards had a mission other than guarding an unarmed, caged gnome."

We hurried down another street. At the corner he made a sharp turn and we broke into a jog. I don't know how he unerringly found his way around almost any city.

As we approached the next corner, he slowed down to a brisk walk...and then stopped. We were standing opposite a quaint shop, with jars of various colors and shapes aligning shelves. Sir Locke turned his cloak inside out, handed me his pack, lute, and sword. He instructed me to wait until the "way was clear" then to join him in the store. He ruffled his hair and put on a big smile. He had transformed from a super-focused serious sleuth into what looked for all intent and purposes like a young human boy (as long as the hood covered his ears).

When the door started to open, he started skipping (yes, really skipping) toward the shop. As the guard exited the store, Sir Locke bumped into him and let out a gleeful laugh as if it was the funniest thing in the world. The guard took a swipe at him with the back of his hand. Sir Locke easily slipped below the swing and disappeared into the establishment. I watched as the guard grumbled something about annoying children, straightened his tunic, and headed off.

I waited until he was out of sight to join my friend.

"What exactly were the potions?" He was already deep into a conversation with the owner.

"Here's me ledger. All legitimate sales I tell ya. I'm a reputable alchemist you know."

I doubted this, but Sir Locke was fond of telling me that just because you were a crook didn't mean you weren't honest.

"Thank you, good man." Sir Locke turned to me. "Latswin, please pay the man."

I wasn't sure what my five gold pieces had bought us since I didn't see any exchange of goods.

"Why…"

"Information is expensive my friend. Other than land, it's the best investment you can make."

With that I paid the sum and we left the shop.

"We have to get to the trial," Sir Locke said, moving quickly again. He took up his brisk pace heading back the way we had come.

"I thought there wasn't going to be a trial?" I said trying to keep up and keep my wits about me, but once again failing not to ask questions.

"Don't believe everything someone tells you my dear Latswin. I've learned that information given freely is usually a lie."

"But…"

"There is always a trial of some sort, especially in a city of this size and status. This is the capital, not some backwater town."

We reached the arena in time to hear the announcement for intermission. We hurried in and found our way to the Office of the Master of the Games. The Master of the Games (also known as the Games Master) was a formidable looking human named Dunkirk

Devonshire. He looked like he could have been a gladiator himself. He had a patch over his left eye, but other than that he looked to be in exceptional health. He was gesturing to the magistrate to sit when we crashed the party.

"Whoa now," the magistrate started as he stood back up. He had almost plumped his butt into the chair but on seeing us enter the room, he found his feet again. The ever-present guards by his side were stationed by the door and raised their hands to stop our entry.

"Kind sir, Master Devonshire, if we may," Sir Locke began. "We represent the defendant, Gobnac Gilshire."

Sir Locke spoke with an eloquence I had never heard before. Regardless of his inability to make an audience laugh (more than once), he was becoming an excellent bard.

The Games Master seemed to be no-nonsense.

"Let them in. I will hear as many sides to this story as there are."

"There's only two sides, the truth and their lies," the magistrate whined (I'm sorry, I'm usually not so vindictive, but I genuinely disliked this man).

"We'll see," Devonshire said.

The Master of the Games was like the general manager, director, and producer of the city's gladiatorial games. As such he had considerable power. The games were the greatest attraction in the capital, was responsible for bringing in over 70% of the annual income to the city's merchants as well as for the city government. The arena was considered his sovereign territory. That, coupled with gnomes being treated as second-class citizens, meant that there would likely not be a real trial. None of us were considered actual citizens of the empire.

Once again, and I write this with all humility, I did an outstanding job of keeping my mouth shut. I had to trust in my friend to win the day. There was too much at stake for me to risk making a mess of it.

But my good friend, my childhood friend, my champion of truth and justice, did nothing. He pulled up a chair, offered it to me (my feet *were* tired) and then walked over to the impressive shelf of books.

Devonshire sat in his chair, behind his desk, and lit a pipe. I looked around wondering where his guards were...I thought everyone of importance had body-guards.

"Alright Barrols, what's your case?"

The "Right Honorable Filmore Barrols," the magistrate of the 6th district in the capital city of Grimstone, began his monologue. I don't know what else to call it. It lasted nearly thirty minutes and I refuse to share his ramblings as I will not be party to documenting false allegations against my relative. I will only share the pertinent details of the accusation.

"Gobnac Tadyddwiem Densnag Gilshire, poisoned the Champion Tyann Rit so that he'd be in a weakened state during the match and thereby would lose to the challenger. But, Gobnac obviously messed up the dosage and gave him too much, killing him."

I couldn't help but snort when he used the word "obviously." I immediately threw my hands over my mouth as if to pull it back in. I glanced at Sir Locke, expecting his admonishing glare, but his eyes and lips both smiled.

"Evidence Filmore?" Devonshire asked.

He pulled a vial from his pocket. It was full of a red liquid.

"Exhibit A - a vial of the poison used by Gobnac to kill our champion. It was found in his house, just an hour ago when we searched it." He handed the vial to Devonshire.

"Exhibit 2 - Gilshire won over 10,000 gold by betting on the challenger!"

"Where did you find that vial?" Finally, Sir Locke spoke up. He sounded patient, even conspiratorial, as if he wanted to help.

"In Gobnac's house."

"Where in the house?" still calm and relaxed.

"I don't know...in his bedroom. Or maybe the kitchen." Barrols was starting to become irritated.

"So, *you* didn't find it?" Sir Locke asked apologetically.

I stole a look over at Devonshire. He was watching this exchange with curiosity.

"No. I don't do that sort of thing. My men, one of my men found it."

"Oh. It's red?"

"Yes! Just like the red you found on Tyann Rit's mouth." He seemed to just then realize that Sir Locke wasn't on his side.

"Does it smell of Death Lily?"

"Yes! Just like the smell from…" he fell silent.

"Oh, please don't stop now," Devonshire said.

"It was the same as what this gnome found on Rit's mouth," he said, pointing to Sir Locke.

"Funny, I never told you about that. Actually, the only time I mentioned any of that was when I visited Gobnac in his cell."

"So, what of it? My guard heard you and when we found the vial we put two and two together and…" the Magistrate tried.

"And got eight." Sir Locke finished it for him.

"Your honor," Sir Locke addressed Devonshire, "I offer you the proven adage that a politician knows how to manipulate the truth…"

"Are you calling me a politician?" Barrols interrupted.

"Definitely not. As far as I can tell, you have no acquaintance with the truth," Sir Locke said.

Barrols seemed satisfied that Sir Locke had retracted his insult.

"You see, Sire, I lied to Gobnac, loud enough for the guards to overhear. When they reported back to the magistrate, he sent one of them to procure a vial of poison so that he could frame his prisoner."

"I never…"

"Actually, you did." Sir Locke pulled out a ledger from his cloak.

"The shopkeeper allowed me to borrow his ledger; he keeps excellent records, your honor." Sir Locke opened the ledger and showed him the purchase record from about an hour ago.

"And if you check the quantity of the vial, you will find that it matches what was sold. Strange that anyone was able to poison Tyann Rit without using up any of the poison." Sir Locke looked over at the Magistrate.

"So what! He still poisoned him! All I know is my man said he found it in Gobnac's place."

"So, you didn't give him instructions and the ten gold pieces to purchase it?"

"Of course not!" The magistrate was losing steam.

"Odd. Seems your guard dropped this note at the apothecary's. It's in your handwriting…" Sir Locke handed the note to Devonshire.

"So what! He still poisoned Tyann Rit!"

"And you know that because…"

"Because he had red, lily-smell stuff in and around his mouth! You said so yourself."

"Perhaps you missed it, I said I lied." Sir Locke let the statement settle before moving on.

"Latswin was asked to determine the cause of death, and unlike myself, has no talent for misinformation. Latswin please describe your findings to the Games Master."

I was surprised to be called upon, but I believe I acquitted myself fairly.

"His lips had a blue tinge to them, a dark blue. His tongue and teeth had a faint dark blue tint also, as if he had been drinking something that tainted them such. His eyes, even in death, were extremely dilated. His skin was warm to the touch, and the temperature increased during my inspection."

"Is that normal?" Devonshire didn't use a lot of words.

"Not at all. He should have been turning cold, and his eyes should have had no dilation. I can guarantee that he was not killed with a Death Lily or any other poison I know of." This was of course true, but I knew very little of any poison. I was just saying what my friend had instructed me to.

"Ha!" The Magistrate shouted at me.

"Barrols!" Devonshire shut him down. "By your own admission, you did no investigation of your own, you fabricated evidence, and you picked out your culprit solely based on the fact that he is a good gambler. It's time for you to be quiet."

"Oh, there's more," Sir Locke offered.

"I can't wait," the Games Master said, and to my surprise, meant it.

"Before we could look over the body, pretty much minutes after Tyann Rit's death, the magistrate arrested Gobnac Gilshire."

"I told you - he bet ten times…" Barrols started and then saw Devonshire looking at him with his one eye and he stopped talking.

"Yes, he bet ten times more than anyone else. 10,000 gold pieces. The question is, how'd the magistrate know that?" My friend paused for effect. "I thought it was strange that he was arrested so quickly. And then I confirmed my suspicions with Gobnac."

The magistrate opened and closed his mouth, but no sound came out.

"The magistrate has a sideline of taking books. At 10 to 1 odds, he was due to lose a sizable sum. Easier to pin the murder on Gobnac then to pay him."

The Games Master actually clapped for Sir Locke. It was an audience of one (the magistrate definitely didn't enjoy the performance), but applause is applause, no matter how small.

"Excellent, young Holgrim!" It seemed Devonshire had a pretty good network. The use of Sir Locke's family name didn't seem to throw my friend off at all. "So, how did our champion die?" he asked. "I have a scheduled execution for tomorrow and I hate to disappoint the people." He seemed to be fighting not to smile when he said this. "Who is to blame?"

"Sire, if you would allow a private audience? This matter requires a little delicacy, of which I don't trust the magistrate, is capable of."

Barrols didn't argue.

We left the room, allowing Sir Locke and the Master of the Games to speak in private. I followed the Right Honorable Filmore Barrols, determined that he would not escape. It was unnecessary - he walked into the spacious foyer, found a chair and slumped into it, dejected and defeated.

After an hour Sir Locke emerged from the room with Devonshire. They were laughing. Devonshire pointed his pipe at me and said, "You have yourself a special friend here, young gnome. Treat him well."

Now I smiled. I knew all would be right again.

The guards took the magistrate into custody and put him into the same cell Gobnac had occupied. Gobnac was given a free night's stay at the arena (they have some of the best high-end accommodations in the city). The next morning the crowd had their spectacle. Not an execution, but an amateur match between "Gobnac the gambler Gilshire" and "The Once Right Honorable Filmore Barrols." They used wood practice swords and Gobnac punished the magistrate quite soundly. The crowd especially liked the part when Gobnac chased the halfling in a circle, swatting his backside with the flat of the sword. Rarely do combatants get serious injury from practice swords, but I heard that Barrols couldn't sit for a week after that. Oh, and he lost his position as magistrate, had to pay off Gobnac's bet, and left the city in humiliation. Needless to say, that day Sir Locke made one loyal friend and one eternal enemy.

But, I am neglecting my duties as chronicler of my friend's prowess.

While Gobnac dined and slept in preparation of his debut in the arena, Sir Locke and I had a quiet dinner in a nearby pub. Finally, I could ask him all of the questions that had been rolling around in my head.

"This was a day of information, misinformation, lies, and more lies," my friend said.

"I have so many questions!"

"Yes, yes, Latswin. But not all at once."

"So, how'd you do it? How'd you know about the poison? How'd you…" I stopped. "Sorry, please, do tell."

"Let's start at the beginning. What did we do first?" he asked

I was tempted to say "travel to the capital" but I knew he meant after Tyann Rit fell in the arena.

"We examined the body. Tip to top and back again. You even smelled his breath," I said.

"Yes, you are correct. That was our first attempt to gather information. Every case is solved through the gathering, nurturing, and interpretation of information."

"But Tyann Rit was dead…"

"Yes. The dead don't lie," he said.

"So, our examination was gathering information?" I asked.

"Yes, and it was good that we had the opportunity to do so. Did you notice anything missing?"

"His mace and shield...wait they were on the table to the side. What was missing?" I couldn't think of anything.

"The wineskin he drank from before and during his match."

"Why would someone take that?"

"Why indeed?" He pulled the mutton off the bone and dipped it in the sauce.

"Because, they wanted a keepsake?" I guessed.

"Unlikely. The manager…"

"Carter Vaughan" I added proudly.

"Yes, Carter Vaughan, ran out to him in the arena and hadn't left his side until we arrived."

"Who took it then?"

"Who indeed?" Another morsel of mutton.

"Well. It had to be Carter then!"

"Excellent Latswin!"

"And he took it because he had poisoned the contents?" I grimaced. "No, if he was the killer, you would have had him arrested. And Rit wasn't poisoned, I pronounced that myself! So why did he take it?"

Only my friend's eyes smiled, revealing his humor at my flailing about.

"Because he did put something in the wineskin. Just not poison. Didn't you recognize the smell from his breath?"

I thought a bit.

"Yes! It was a healing potion. But I figured that was from them trying to revive poor Tyann."

"And the blue color?"

"Not sure. It was another potion. Not a poison, I'm sure of that."

"You were right, good friend." He took the alchemist's ledger from his cloak and put it on the table. "Don't get it dirty," he said between bites.

I wiped my hands carefully before looking through the pages.

"You'll see that Carter Vaughan was a regular customer. He bought two types of potions."

I scanned and found his name in the book multiple times over many years.

"Healing and Haste?" I said, reading the scrawl.

"Yes. He confessed that he had made a personal concoction that he slipped to Tyann before each match. A delicate mix as he put it."

"So, the healing would allow Tyann to take some extra punishment. And the haste?"

"It gave him an edge in speed."

"Did Tyann know?" I asked.

"I don't believe so. The manager didn't think so. Tyann had a reputation for honesty and fairness - I doubt he would have approved of being juiced."

"Juiced?" I hadn't heard this term before.

"That's what Carter called it."

"Ah, but that doesn't explain his death. If Carter had been slipping him this delicate mix for years, what went wrong this time?" I asked.

"That my dear Latswin is an excellent question. The answer to which may be the saddest of tragedies I have ever heard." He pushed back from the table a bit. He lounged back, putting his feet up on the table. He cradled a mug of herbal tea in his lap. He refused to drink anything stronger, saying it dulled his wits.

"Turns out that Carter was worried for his fighter. The juicing was no big deal, they all did something akin to it. But this time he gave Tyann an extra booster of haste because he was afraid he had lost a step."

"And that killed…" I interrupted.

"No. Carter swears that it would take much more than he gave him to cause a problem. Like overheating to the point of death...something about the body not coping. And the alchemist agreed."

"So…"

"Well there was a bit more administered. In fact, Tyann Rit digested ten times the normal dosage, way past what's safe" he said.

"The manager?"

"No, as I said he only gave him a tiny boost...probably double his normal dose."

"Then...oh. No. No, Locke."

He nodded slowly. He let me spell it out.

"The wife? Madam Rit? She slipped him a potion of haste?"

"Yes, you'll see her name in the ledger two days ago."

Sir Locke sipped his tea.

I found her name. Bidde Rit. And the day after that another name I recognized.

"Oh no. That's too sad, Locke" the realization almost made me lose my appetite.

"Yes. His daughter and wife both feared that he wouldn't win his last match. Not because of any monetary loss - he was getting paid the same, win or lose. They loved him and wanted him to go out on top. But neither of them *believed* in him. Both secretly drugged him to give him an advantage. And the combination of the three; the manager, his wife, and his daughter, killed him."

"Do they know?" I asked.

"I didn't tell them. I think each thinks they may have been at fault, and feel guilty. Probably they'll keep the secret to their own graves."

"That's so sad," I said.

He sat and drank his tea. I finished off my meal. We spent the time in quiet contemplation.

Time moved slowly.

"So, what have you learned Latswin?" Sir Locke asked.

"You said it was a case of information and misinformation?"

"Yes. All cases are built upon information - good and bad. False and true," he said.

I nodded encouragingly.

"The detective gathers good information as we did from the victim himself, his manager, his wife, and his daughter."

"And Gobnac!" I offered.

"Yes, and Gobnac. We also gathered bad information. Mostly from the magistrate. But he also provided us with some good information."

"Like what?" I asked incredulously. "The bad was obvious - he pretty much lied every time he opened his mouth! What good information did he provide?"

"He told us that he arrested Gobnac. Which was true...and by announcing it before we even knew how Tyann died, he revealed a lot."

"Well, we also provided misinformation…" I said, reflecting.

"Very good my friend. We definitely did. Lies can be a great tool for getting at the truth."

We sat in silence for a long time.

"I don't think I said thank you." I said finally.

"Nope. But friends don't have to say thanks."

"True." I pushed away from the table and added my feet to the table. A waitress started clearing the table.

"Thank you," I said to my friend.

"You're welcome," the waitress said, thinking I was talking to her.

I was going to explain, but then I noticed Sir Locke smiling and understood that not all misinformation needed to be corrected.

The End

Book Three

The Case of the Missing Crown

a Sir Locke the gnome mystery

The Case of the Missing Crown

By Latswin Gilshire, Cleric

It is with great pleasure that I finally get to tell the tale of how my good friend, nay, my *best friend,* Sir Locke was knighted by King Meryur. As I have explained before, the "knighthood" was more akin to being awarded the key to the city. But, that does not lessen the significance of my friend's abilities to solve mysteries, or the value that others put on his assistance, in such matters.

It was shortly after the Autumn Gladiatorial Games in Grimstone, that my friend and I found ourselves traveling to Taedmorden, the unofficial capital city for gnomes. There we met the King of the Gnomes, and my friend received his well-deserved knighthood.

It was at the Gladiatorial Games where Locke saved my cousin Gobnac, from wrongful persecution (which would have surely led to wrongful execution) at the hands of a dastardly halfling, with the unenviable name of Filmore Barrols. It was in gratitude that my cousin, who already had gifted me tickets to the Games, celebrated his exoneration with a lavish party for Sir Locke and I. His beneficence didn't stop there; he added to all of this by testifying to Sir Locke's genius in a letter to King Meryur. This testimony, along with the accounts of his help to the Mayor of Little Thoracia, our home town, resulted in Sir Locke receiving an appointment with the king. A royal audience!

Yes, king is mostly a ceremonial title. And yes, there is no palace or castle. But we gnomes are not that pretentious a lot anyway. The king has a very nice manor and visitors can look at the crown, scepter, and sword, on display in a room off the main entrance. The king is of "royal" blood and the duties of royalty are passed down through blood, so it's fairly substantial. Well, there was never a Gnome Kingdom or Empire like the current Dragon Empire; there has never been a gnome army or militia even. But King Meryur can trace his lineage back further than any other gnome - so his family has been acknowledged as the oldest in known existence. Making him the king.

And it's good for the tourism trade.

Cousin Gobnac sprung his good news on us the day we were to leave.

"You must detour to Taedmorden on your way home, Latswin," he insisted.

"Why? There's not much to see."

"Well, there's the King of the Gnomes. He's a great fellow. Actually, he's a friend of mine."

"And?" I did not relish the idea of losing a day's worth of travel.

"He always prepares a lavish spread for guests, and I told him you'd be coming. So, you will get special treatment, as well as a good meal, and nice lodgings."

The food *did* sound good. And it *was* a natural midway point back to Little Thoracia. I definitely liked the idea of a comfortable bed after a few days on the road.

"But…" I started to protest. I didn't think Sir Locke would want to stop.

Gobnac pulled me aside and told me of his secret. He said chances were extremely good that Locke would be knighted for the work he did for the mayor, and then for saving his life. It wasn't guaranteed, but he was highly confident that the audience would result in such.

I could in no way be a hindrance to my friend receiving such an honor.

"I'll convince Locke to go!" I said.

It was easier than I thought. My friend seemed to have a wanderlust. A compulsion to adventure out in the world. He was always willing to meet new people, new creatures, to learn everything about anything, and anything about everything.

It would prove to be a challenge to our friendship, soon enough.

We reached Taedmorden after four days on the road from Grimstone. It was a welcome sight to my sore feet and underfed belly. We spent that night in an inn. We would visit the king the next day. Our appointment was for any day in the next month, at noon. It was impossible to predict how long it would take to travel across the country.

We arrived at 11:30 (Locke always preferred being early to being late).

At the door, I noticed a sign above the tour schedule (carved into a wood plaque) that simply said *NO*. I couldn't hide my disappointment. The greeter sitting beside the sign, an elderly gnome, noticed.

"Sorry, young fella. No tours today."

"Why not?" I asked.

"Dunno. Not my job. But we haven't had a tour for near on a week now. Sad really, with it being tourist season and all."

"We're here for an appointment with the king," I said. I felt like I needed to say something.

"Go on in then," he said.

On entering, we were greeted by another gnome. He shuffled along, leading us past the exhibit room to the waiting room. The exhibit room had two doors; one barred, like a prison cell door, and behind that, one of solid wood. The wooden door would normally be open, so tourists could see into the room, but no tours meant no viewing.

While we waited, I fidgeted nervously. I paced the room a few times, admiring the paintings on the wall. There were 11 in all. Each depicted one of the past gnome kings. Each wore the crown, held a scepter in their left hand and a sword in their right. Well, all but one who had the sword in his left and scepter in his right. Some were seated, some standing. One was actually sitting astride a saddled mastiff hound. I looked at the names and years of reign absently. My friend spent the time drawing in his book. He had taken to documenting everything, using his better-than-decent skill with charcoal and paper.

At 11:50 the doors to the king's study opened and a disheveled looking halfling came out, with the king right behind him. The halfling went to the nearest painting and said something to the king. The king removed the painting and handed it to his visitor. They shook hands and the halfling headed out.

The king turned toward us with a smile.

"You must be Latswin Gilshire!" He said. He had a deep, booming voice.

I shook his hand, speechless.

"And you must be the gnome I've heard so much about. A bit of fame is attaching itself to you." Locke shook his hand and gave a slight bow at the same time.

"Sinben Locke Ariji Umji Merfiz Holgrim, but you prefer 'Locke,' right?" the king asked.

"Yes, Sire," Locke replied.

"No need for that. That's for the tourists. *Meryur* will do just fine."

I could see why my cousin liked this gnome.

Inside the study, there was an old hound dog curled up in a patch of sunlight on the floor, and a young gnomish girl, no more than six years old, rocking in a small chair.

"Gentleman, my daughter, Calliope. She likes to sit in on matters of state." He winked at us. Calliope stood up, did a perfect curtsey, and then flopped back into her rocker.

Locke and I both returned the gesture, giving a deep bow.

The king motioned to chairs that were well worn from visitors seeking advice.

"So, I hear that you have done some pretty impressive things," the king said to Locke.

"You flatter me, Your Highness," Locke said, ignoring the king's suggestion to call him Meryur.

"Nonsense! Gobnac assures me that you saved his life."

"That's true, Your Highness," I said. "And Locke also solved a nasty little case of blackmail and extortion in our home town."

"Yes, I've heard." He picked up a letter from his desk. "Urimop wrote me a letter extolling your abilities. He said that you ferreted out the culprit in one night."

"It was amazing," I said. Locke only looked around the room. He smiled at Calliope.

"And according to Gobnac, you uncovered a dishonest magistrate and saved him from a wrongful public execution."

"All true," I said proudly.

"It was nothing, really.   All elementary reasoning." Locke said.

"Would you be willing to give me a demonstration of your talents?"   I feared the king was referring to my friend's bardic performance.   This might change the king's perception of my friend.   I was glad to see that Locke had not brought his lute with him.

Before Locke could reply, the elderly servant knocked and opened the door.

"Sire, young Calliope's friends are arriving."

She looked at her father. "Must I?"

"Of course.   It's your weekly playdate, now go be a good hostess."

"But I want to see…"

"And goblins want to rule the world.   We all have duties and responsibilities, go see to yours," he said with a smile.

She got out of her chair and started heading toward the door.

"Ah hmpf."   The king cleared his throat.

Without missing a beat, Calliope turned smoothly, changed direction, and ran over to her father.   She gave him a kiss on the cheek, and then ran off to her playdate.

"She must find you fascinating.   She never misses her playdates."

When the door was closed behind her, the king returned to his request.

"So, how about that demonstration?"

I could tell that Locke wanted to protest.   He wanted to say he wasn't a performer.   That he was a detective.   But being a bard meant that he was most definitely a performer, and he'd have to get used to this stage as much as he was now used to reciting poems, singing songs, or telling jokes.

"Sire…" the king held up his finger. "Meryur," Locke began again. "My dear friend's cousin, Gobnac, as a gesture of thanks, asked you to knight me. He not only asked you for this small favor but sent some coin along as well, to help sway you to the cause." The king looked at Locke, amused.

"Go on. I could have figured that out, and I'm *not* a detective."

"But, you are hesitating, because the ceremony requires all three artifacts." Locke now spoke slowly. "The royal crown, the scepter, and the sword. All symbols of your station as king of the gnomes. And you don't have all three any longer. There has been a theft."

The king leaned forward.

"It was stolen about a week ago, and you have given up hope of finding the thief, or recovering the crown, so you've arranged to have a replacement made, at great expense."

The king was speechless.

"I can solve the mystery, if you like."

When the king didn't react, he added, "And save you a bit of coin."

The king stood up abruptly and headed to the doors. He swung them open and called for one of his servants. After a quick and animated conversation, he returned to the room.

"Amazing. And you figured all of that out, by, what? How did you know all of that?"

"It was actually rather simple, but if you would indulge me, I'd like to recover your crown first. Time may be of the essence." On this cue, I stood up. I headed toward the door. I was not a bard, and had no interest in being on stage, but being Locke's friend required me to have a little sense of the theatrical. I swung the doors open again. As he swept by me, he said loud enough for the king to hear. "Come Latswin, the gauntlet has been thrown down, and we have not a moment to waste." I closed the door behind us. I hoped it had the dramatic flair my friend deserved.

"So, where to next?" I asked.

"Information is the key, as always, Latswin. And the best place to find information is…"

"The constabulary? The cranks and pranks log book?" I asked. I had a very good memory and I had learned a lot helping my friend on previous cases.

"No, not this time."

"So, the wife? Perhaps the daughter? Are we going to an apothecary again?" This made Locke laugh.

"My dear Latswin, you must learn the concepts behind the moves. Not memorize the opening as if to play it by rote."

I knew he was using a Dragon Chess metaphor. I had yet to beat him at that infernal game.

"We ask those who have the answers, even though they rarely know what they know."

"Thanks for clearing that up," I said a little testily.

"Servants hear and see everything, but they don't usually know the value of what it is they witness."

"Ah," I said.

"Children too."

"So, I was right about the daughter?" I was hoping for a one-out-of-three accuracy. I had thrown the daughter into my guess not because I thought Calliope might know something, but because in our previous case the daughter was involved. I admit I was fishing for any small morsel, but mangy dogs shouldn't be picky about the scraps they get.

"Yes, you were right." Locke said this with a smile. "Have I ever told you about the concept of the broken clock?"

"Ha. Ha. Ha," I said. We both smiled.

As we exited the study, a servant approached us. He was the elderly one that had brought us in.

"Will you be…" he started.

"Working for the king today. Can we go to the kitchen?" Locke asked.

We found out his name was Gueld, and he had been working for the royal family since he was a youth. He was now the head servant, and was thinking about retirement. We learned how many children, grandchildren, and great grandchildren he had. All of this in the time it took to get to the kitchen. I learned two things; when you become a co-worker, the staff opens up easily, and it can take a long time to walk forty feet if you shuffle the whole way.

As we entered the kitchen, Gueld introduced us to the cooks.

"Ladies, this is Misters Holgrim and Gilshire. They are working for the king today." He stopped abruptly and turned to us. "What exactly are you doing for the king?"

"We're investi…" I started but Locke cut me off. "We're running a few errands. He said we could get a bite to eat first? We missed lunch."

I was shocked. Not about the request for food - of that I was thankful. We had only had a second breakfast before arriving for our appointment and my stomach had wondered more than once when it was going to get some food. But Locke, once on a case, rarely stopped to do anything unrelated to solving it. And food was never a priority before.

One of the cooks grumbled under her breath, but the other one, a cheerful gnome, made a sweeping motion with her hand, inviting us to sit at the large table they used for preparing food. It doubled for the staff's dining table.

"Hope you're hungry. We have lots of food, as the young'uns didn't show up today."

We sat as she started bringing over bowls of food.

"How many usually attend the playdate?" Locke asked as he picked up a fork.

"The missus has six saplings that come to play. Two girls and four boys. But today only that pimply one showed up."

"Berta!" The grumpy cook turned away from the pot she was working on to admonish her coworker.

Berta smiled at us conspiratorially, "He has a crush on our young missus. He never misses a playdate."

"Except last week," Grumpy corrected her.

"His family attended the Autumn Gladiatorial Games in Grimstone," Berta whispered.

I took another spoonful of pot pie. It was delicious.

"So, less work this week?" Locke asked. He didn't seem to be eating his dish.

"Not really. We have to start cooking well before they get here. It would have been wasted, but for the two of you." She smiled at Locke. I wondered if he realized she was flirting with him.

"Less cleaning though, right? Seven little ones can make a big mess…" he offered.

"Nah. They never play inside. They'd get in the way of tourists. They have their own area in the back yard where they play. They even picnic out there unless the weather's lousy. Which is rare."

The grumpy one came over and tried to take my bowl away. I guessed she was the one who cleaned the pots and pans while the cheery one was the actual cook. I begrudgingly let her take my bowl. She looked at Locke's and saw he hadn't touched it. When she turned away, Locke slid the bowl over to me.

"What kind of errands are you two doing?" Berta asked.

"Well, we were told something went missing lately." He said, whispering it as if it were a secret.

Berta leaned over close to Locke.

"Yes! This time the king's crown! In the middle of the day! One second it was there and the next it was gone!"

"Hmph." Grumpy added. "No one noticed until after the lunch break."

"Tours are in the morning and afternoon. Gueld noticed it missing as he was leading a group and immediately canceled the tour. They had to refund them their fees." Berta was hovering over Locke. She put two more bowls in front of him. One was a pastry, and the other a pudding. She forgot to give me anything, which was okay as I was still finishing up Locke's pot pie.

"What was taken before?" Locke asked.

I have to admit I was surprised by the question. I had totally missed that she had said *this time*.

"Nothing valuable. Junk really. And never from inside the manor," Grumpy said, not turning around. She seemed to be speaking to the pots, pans, and dirty dishes. She came back and took my bowl again. Locke slid me his pudding.

"What kind of junk?" Locke asked.

"A copper coin, a cheap bracelet, and a comb."

"Two forks and a spoon." Grumpy added.

"One of the kids may have pocketed those," Berta said.

"It must have been a pretty crazy scene when Gueld reported the crown missing," Locke said. He passed me his pastry.

"Stupid constable. He couldn't find his thumb if it was stuck up his nose." Grumpy said to the pots.

"We searched all over. When we couldn't find it, we had the constable come over. He had three men help him. They spent more time grilling us than looking for it...as if any of us would take it!"

"Stupid gnome." Grumpy said as if confirming Berta's story.

"Did they question the kids?" Locke asked.

"Why would they do that?" Grumpy asked.

"They may have seen something..." Locke said. Seemed that even the staff dismissed the kids.

"Nah, they had gone home already. Someone probably sent them away to keep them out of the way. They usually play until dusk, but they were all gone by the time the constable got here."

"Stupid constable."

I deduced that there was something going on with the grumpy one and the constable. I made a mental note to share that with Locke later. I thought it might be critical to the case in some way.

Locke patted his stomach as if he were full.

"Thanks for lunch." He stood up.

Berta smiled again at Locke. She pulled back her hair from her face.

"Will you be here for pre-dinner?" she asked. She didn't seem to notice that Locke hadn't actually eaten anything. I finished the pastry and stood up.

"Most likely," Locke said.

"Thank you," I said. Berta didn't seem to hear me.

"Hmph," Grumpy said, not looking around.

We went back out the way we came.

Locke spotted Calliope, sitting halfway up the stairs to the second floor. Her elbows were on her knees. Her hands in little fists, supported her pouting chin. He walked over to her and bowed, then sat next to her. I didn't want to make her feel uncomfortable, so I went about examining the paintings in the hall.

"M'lady," he said. She giggled. "Where are your playmates?"

"They stood me up."

"Not everyone. Who was it that showed up?" I found it amazing how he remembered so many tiny details.

"Hmph. Percy. We can't play with just two of us."

"What games do you play?" Locke asked. I expected him to ask about the theft, maybe see if she had noticed anyone lurking about, hiding in the shadows or looking suspicious.

"Hide and Seek, King of the Mountain, Demons and Daggers. Just normal stuff," she said.

"Can you help us?"

She perked up.

"Sure!"

"Can you give us a tour of the manor?" Locke asked.

Calliope seemed a little disappointed, but she got up and started down the stairs. At the bottom she turned toward the main rooms.

"No, I'm sorry. I meant the outside grounds."

This seemed to make her a little happier. She obviously liked being outside and wasn't excited about being an unofficial tour guide.

We went outside, and Locke made a point of looking at windows and doors, as if determining how someone could sneak inside.

When we had circled the entire manor, he asked Calliope, "So where do you play your games?"

She skipped over to an area of the backyard. Even I could see that this was where they played. Besides the sandpit in one corner, the grass was worn away in different spots. Probably from where they played Demons and Daggers. There were two low tables at the north end of the area, where they must eat their lunch. The western side was lined with hedges. This area was across from a side door in the manor.

"Are you allowed past the hedges?" Locke asked, approaching them.

"No. We all have to stay on the grounds."

Locke got on his hands and knees and crawled along the boundary.

"You're going to get wet," Calliope said.

She was right. Across from where the sandpit was, the ground was wetter. Locke ended up with wet hands and knees. Calliope giggled.

"Told you," she said.

Locke pushed back the brush a little.

"What's through there?"

"A pond. We skate on it in the winter."

Locke stood up.

"Would you like to help me get the crown back for your dad?"

Calliope didn't say anything. She just looked at Locke. I wasn't sure what was going on.

"You can find it?" she finally asked.

"Sure."

She ran over to Locke and hugged him. She was crying.

I looked at Locke, confused.

"Let's go fishing," he said.

We found Gueld and gathered some equipment. One wicker basket, 20 feet of rope, an animal cage (this we had to get from a neighbor), and a ball. I was still confused.

"What's all this for?" I asked. Calliope looked as curious as me.

"Well, the rope is to catch our thief. The cage is to hold him. The basket is to collect the spoils and the ball is for you and Calliope to play with." Calliope and I looked at each other.

We went out to the play area and Locke put the wicker basket and cage by the tables. He took the rope over to the hedge where he had gotten wet, and spent at least forty minutes playing with it while we watched. Finally, he backed away. Whatever he had done, he had buried it under the wet ground so it was hard to see the rope. Two or three feet away, the rope continued out of the mud. He carefully extended the rope, smoothing it out, until he was by the table with us.

"Latswin, I need five gold pieces."

I was still confused, but I opened my purse and before I could take out the coins, Locke took the bag, and turned it over on the table. He quickly captured them, not letting any fall to the ground. He picked through the coins, taking three silver instead of gold.

"I thought you wanted five gold?" I asked.

"These will do better," he said. "Do you mind putting the rest back?"

I didn't mind.

He took the three coins over to the sandpit, and laid them carefully on the ground where the sand stopped and the grass started. When he came back he handed Calliope the ball.

"Okay, your turn. I want you to play with Latswin. I want you two to make a lot of noise. Happy sounds. Laughter would be great. Make it sound like all of your playmates are here. And whatever you do, do *not* look toward the sandpit. Can you two do that?"

I was not in the best shape, and while traveling from Little Thoracia to Grimstone, and back again, was great exercise, that little girl literally ran rings around me. I'm not sure what the ball was for. She skipped, hopped and jumped around me, singing, laughing and yelling. All I could do was sing an old children's song I knew and try to keep from fainting. Watching her was exhausting.

About ten minutes in, I heard a loud croaking noise. It was a mix between a toad's love call, and the sound an animal makes when its leg is caught in a trap. We both turned and looked where Locke told us not to. The bushes were shaking and Locke was reeling in the rope like he was pulling in a large fish. He kept walking toward the bush line while pulling in the rope, not allowing any slack.

"Croak! Croak!" Something was on the end of his rope that didn't want to be.

Finally, it emerged from the bushes. A large frog man. Later I learned they're called bullywogs[9], but I had never seen one. It looked like a two-foot tall frog with clothes on. It was trying to get its leg out of the rope. It batted at it, scratched at it with its hands and finally was biting at it. But Locke's trap was too well designed. This frog man was a little bigger than Calliope, but she didn't seem scared at all. She walked closer to it and in a soothing voice said, "It's ok. It's ok. We won't hurt you."

"Croak," was the only answer it gave.

---

[9] A bullywog is an amphibious humanoid creature found in wetlands

We were able to get it into the cage without too much fuss. Once it saw Locke and I, it seemed to resign itself to being captured. Actually, I don't think it was scared of us; gnomes aren't by nature a scary lot. But it was more than likely Calliope's reassurances, and kind face, that calmed it down.

"So, this is the thief?" I asked.

"Sort of," Locke said.

"How are we going to get it to tell us where the crown is?" I asked.

"Croak." It seemed the frogman agreed.

"It already has, we just have to listen."

Calliope and I looked at each other. We both shrugged in unison and then laughed. It seemed that I had found a kindred spirit.

The bullywog was turned over to Gueld, who found a collar to use instead of the cage. The ladies in the kitchen fed it (turns out it liked minced meat pies) while Locke, Calliope, and I followed the bullywog's fresh trail from the play area back to the pond. There was a small dugout near the water. The ground was wet but Calliope didn't seem to mind. She made five trips back and forth into the dugout, bringing out the treasures our frog man had collected. Now I saw why we had a wicker basket. There were many more things than we had heard about. Some were kid's toys, some shiny coins, trinkets, and knick knacks. And she also retrieved the crown.

All of the items were surprisingly clean. Even so, all items were washed thoroughly by the king's staff.

That evening we had dinner with the king and his daughter.

"I must know how you did it, young man," the king demanded.

"Mostly through observation and reasoning. Anyone could have done it." Locke began.

"I doubt that. How did you figure it all out? How did you know about the theft, or how long ago it occurred? Why were you so confident that you could recover the crown?" I ate while the king and Calliope looked at Locke with admiration. I knew exactly how they felt. I let the king ask all my usual questions.

It was fun, watching someone else be amazed.

"As I said, it really was quite simple." Locke put down his fork and knife. He took a sip of water (he still refused to drink ale, mead, or wine). He stood up and began explaining. This was Sir Locke at his best. His face flushed with excitement, and you could see the fire of discovery in his eyes.

"I knew something had caused the tours to be canceled. And your man outside mentioned that it had been a week since a tour had been given. When we came in, the artifact viewing room had the inner door closed, keeping visitors from seeing that a sacred item was missing...no other real reason to have the door closed. The only reason to have the barred door would be so onlookers, tourists, could see the prized items, but couldn't touch them."

The king put his arm around his daughter. They both were obviously enjoying Locke's reveal.

"When the artisan…"

"How did you know he was an artist?" Calliope asked.

"M'lady, you have to agree, the gentleman was obviously such by his choice of clothes. And if not his wardrobe, then the specks of paint on his hands and face," Locke said kindly.

"And in his hair," Calliope added.

"Good observation M'lady!"

She beamed. I knew how that felt too. Getting a compliment from Locke was always enjoyable.

"Well, when he left, he took one of the paintings with him. Not one of the older ones where the royal artifacts were poorly represented. No, he took one where the items were prominent and the detail was exquisite." I thought back. I had been the one looking at the paintings, but I couldn't tell you anything about them. Except that one king (which one, I don't remember) was sitting on a large hound. I again marveled at my friend's power of observation, when he seemed to be totally unaware of his surroundings.

"So, I reasoned that you had given up the search, and decided to have one recreated."

"But, it could have been the scepter, or sword. How'd you know it was the crown?" the king asked.

"I must confess, Your Highness. I found out during my interrogation."

"Who'd you interrogate? Not poor old Gueld. He's been with my family since…"

"No, not Gueld, Your Highness. You." Locke looked apologetic. "When I mentioned that you needed each of the three artifacts, I listed each, slowly and deliberately. I watched to see how you reacted. When I mentioned the crown, your eyes fell. But when I listed the scepter and sword, you regained your composure. It was a small tell."

Once again, I realized I was holding my breath, worried how the king would react.

"Well done! I never was a good liar," the king said.

"An admirable trait for a king," Locke said. "Or a princess."

They looked at each other again and they shared another quick hug.

"But, how did you know you could recover it? And so fast? So easily?"

"Sire, could my friend Latswin here, possibly have royal blood? You and he both ask more questions than I can answer at one time." Locke said as he put a hand on my shoulder. I was still eating and this made me nearly choke. I was sure we'd be thrown out for such rudeness.

But, my friend was becoming a true bard. He had read his audience better than I could. The king and his daughter looked at each other, and laughed out loud.

"Fair enough young Holgrim, fair enough. Go on."

"I reasoned that I could recover it because I didn't think it was stolen for its value. I estimate it is only worth about ten gold pieces?"

"Not even that. It's not real gold and the gems are fakes. It's just a prop," the king said.

"Yes, I reasoned so, based on the minor amount of security, and the lack of urgency by the constabulary to find the thief. That, and the fact that the artisan could make a replica as fast as you were hoping, told me the theft was not one for monetary gain. So, it had to be something else."

Locke circled the table.

"I learned that there had been a few other minor thefts, but none from inside. And, the other thefts were all magpie items, versus things of value. So, I reasoned that we could catch such a thief, and recover the items."

The king looked contemplative.

"But, that bullywog couldn't have come into the house, and…" The king began.

"But, he could fit through the bars, he's as small as a child!" I said. I had finished my meal, and was ready to help my good friend.

"Yes Latswin, but the king is correct. If it was the bullywog, the floor would have been soaked, and there were plenty of other shiny things he could have taken, well before finding the crown."

"So, how did he get the crown?" I was a little irritated.

"Yes, how?" The king agreed.

"Indeed, that's a good question." Locke said, sitting down next to Calliope.

"You can tell him, he won't get mad," Locke said.

"Are you sure?" Calliope asked.

"Have I been wrong yet?" Locke asked.

"I took it, Daddy." Calliope said. "We were playing king of the mountain, and Jimy Monsbort said that I couldn't be the king of the mountain because I was a girl. He said it would be different if I had a crown or something. So, I took the crown."

The king looked at her a little sternly.

"But, I was going to return it before the afternoon tours started. I promise."

"I believe you," the king said.

"Yeah but that bullywog took it while we were arguing about who could wear it next. When we looked around for it, it was gone!"

"And, you were too scared to tell me?" The king asked.

Calliope nodded, tears running down her face.

"Come here, my child." He pulled his daughter into his arms.

"I'm sorry Daddy," she sobbed.

"No reason to apologize dear. I'm the one who is sorry. If you are scared to tell me the truth, then I have failed you as a father." He pulled her back so she was at arm's length. He looked her in the eyes. "I'm sorry honey. Please forgive me."

She nodded and then started crying again. He pulled her in close and they hugged each other for a while.

Locke actually sat down and started eating. He passed me his pudding.

When they had gathered themselves, the king wiped his daughter's face. Then they smiled at each other and hugged again. He picked her up and put her on his lap, they both faced Locke.

"How'd you know Mr. Holgrim?" she asked.

Locke looked at Calliope with affection. I think he truly liked this little girl.

"Your friends. I hear they're pretty consistent, never missing a playdate. But all of them skipped today."

"Except Pimply Percy," I said. And then regretted it. I looked at Calliope and the king, and was ready to grovel, when they both started laughing.

"That boy," the king said, shaking his head.

"Yes, except for young master Percy," Locke said, looking at me, like my mom did when I said a bad word. "He showed up, but that's because he wasn't here last week when the crown went missing. He had no idea that anything was amiss."

"Yup. And still doesn't." Calliope said smiling.

"So, I reasoned that they all were avoiding your playdate, and the most logical reason was that they were worried about getting into trouble. I just needed you to confirm it for me Calliope, which you were nice enough to do."

"But I didn't…" she began.

"Sure you did. The way you sped up when we passed the display room on the way outside, the way you avoided the sand area where you left the crown, and the way you avoided my eyes whenever I mentioned the theft."

"I guess I'm not a good liar either. And that's good right?" Calliope asked.

"Yes, that's very good," I said. I was so proud of my friend that day, that I decided to write his exploits so others could learn of him. This was the case that convinced me to become his biographer.

That next morning, the king knighted my best friend. He said he wanted to do it in front of the whole town. Fifty or so townsfolk showed up and at least twenty tourists; word that the tours had reopened spread quickly. We heard it was one of the biggest turnouts in years for a knighting.

It was that day, that my best friend in the whole world, stopped being Sinben Locke Ariji Umji Merfiz Holgrim, and became Sir Locke the Gnome.

The End

Book Four

The Case of the Restless Spirit

The Adventures of Sir Locke the gnome

The Case of the Restless Spirit

By Latswin Gilshire, Cleric

Sir Locke was not unfamiliar with being hired for his investigative powers, but this was the first time that he was sought out by strangers. Therefore, you might say this was our first adventure. In either case, this was definitely the strangest case we've had so far, and one that would change my outlook on life drastically.

We had recently returned from the Autumn Gladiatorial Games, and Sir Locke's official knighting, when we received a visitor. Luckily, I had a week left before my university courses resumed, otherwise I may have missed Sir Locke's fourth case.

We were enjoying a show at the tavern, a Kenku was performing a spirited rendition of some classics.

"So *that's* what a real bard looks like?" I asked, teasing my good friend.

"Yes, she's really good," Sir Locke said.

"She? How can you tell?" A Kenku is a bird-like creature and I couldn't tell the gender.

"Her name is Pluck. I spoke with her between sets. She's very nice and very talented." Sir Locke was watching her closely. For all of his confidence in his investigative powers, he had an equal amount of insecurity around his bardic talents.

I blame the Kenku's performance for allowing the young halfling to take us both by surprise.

"Sir Locke, the gnome?" I realized that it was the second time he had asked.

"Yes, this is Sir Locke," I said. My friend was ignoring the interruption. "How can we help you?"

"Are you Latswin, the cleric?"

"Yes. Who's asking?" The young halfling was modestly dressed, with a healthy layer of road dust.

"My name is Bavo Underfoot. My sister and I need your help."

I have to confess that I did not like this Bavo, from the beginning. I didn't know why, but I didn't like him.

"Why do you think Sir Locke would help you?"

"In truth, I can't think of a reason. We don't have any money to pay him. But if he doesn't…all is lost," he said.

I wanted to feel sorry for him, but I couldn't.

"Well, if you can't think of a reason…"

"Don't be rude, Latswin. Invite the young halfling to join us." Sir Locke didn't look away from the Kenku's performance.

"Please," I said as quietly as I could, motioning to the empty chair.

"Latswin, young Bavo has walked all the way from Virden for our help, offer him some food and drink," Sir Locke said.

"How did you know I came from Virden? Or that I walked?" Bavo asked as he sat down.

I poured our visitor a glass of mead and passed him Locke's untouched plate of mutton and potatoes. The halfling drank the mead greedily, and picked through the food.

Sir Locke didn't answer Bavo's questions. He was still watching the Kenku.

The halfling seemed to realize that Sir Locke was distracted, and decided not to bother him. He softly said to me, "How'd he know?"

"It's what he does," I said. I know it wasn't a *real* answer, but I didn't know how to explain my friend's talents. And I didn't know how Sir Locke knew. I had wondered that myself.

"So, what exactly is your problem?" I asked.

"You probably won't believe me. *I* barely believe it."

Pluck finished her number and took a bow. There was a smattering of cheers, applause, and the sound of copper coins being tossed onto the stage. Locke clapped and then, for the first time, that I could tell, turned to look at the halfling.

"Of course, I'll believe you. It's unlikely you'd travel a full day to tell us lies. How can we help?" Sir Locke said.

This seemed to reassure our guest.

"My twin sister and I…" He stopped. "Our father, our father died last month." He looked around the room, then down at his hands. He put the fork down and moved the plate toward the center of the table.

"He died in poverty, alone, in our family home."

"How did he die?" I asked.

"He was killed by a robber. Broke into the house, and killed him. So senseless. Everyone knew he didn't have anything worth stealing. The constabulary thinks it was a transient."

"So, you want Sir Locke to solve the murder?" I asked.

"No. Well, sure, but that wasn't why…*can* he?"

I looked at Sir Locke, who was leaning back in his chair, watching us. He didn't offer anything, so I continued.

"Maybe," I said. No reaction from Sir Locke. "So why do you need our help?"

"Well, our father always told us that he was going to leave us an inheritance, so we could live better than he did. He told us this since we were little. Our mom died when we were young, and he had to raise us on his own. We never had anything new. No new clothes, furniture, toys…nothing. He worked hard, but we always just got by."

I was starting to feel bad about disliking him.

"All my dad owned was the house. We're trying to sell it so he could give us that inheritance he always wanted." He took a sip of the mead.

"But we can't sell it, no one will buy it. It's a good house, sturdy, well built, and in a good neighborhood."

"So why can't you sell it?" I asked.

He went quiet. He took another sip of his mead.

"Every time we show the house, well, we run into a problem."

"A problem?" I asked, trying to encourage him to get to the point. I couldn't think of something that would be so bad that he couldn't even tell us.

"Yes." Again, he went quiet.

The Kenku was taking the stage again, for another set. Sir Locke obviously didn't want to miss the set.

"What exactly is the problem?" Sir Locke said, giving the young halfling his full attention.

"A ghost." He waited to see how we reacted. When we didn't, that must have been enough to encourage him to continue. "We believe it's our father. But we don't know why his ghost would stop us from selling the house."

"I don't know if…" I started, but Sir Locke interrupted me.

"We'll help," Sir Locke said.

"Thank you. Thank you." Bavo said. His back straightened and for the first time since he approached us, his eyes met ours. I thought he might cry, but he breathed in deep, and took a full swallow of mead instead.

It was a full day's journey to Virden. Bavo wouldn't spend the night in Little Thoracia, saying he didn't want to leave his sister alone any longer than absolutely necessary. He took a short nap and headed back. Sir Locke wanted to do some research and spent most of the night reading everything he could find on ghosts and hauntings. We headed out to Virden the next morning, at dawn.

"So, how did you know where Bavo was from? And that he walked all day?" I asked.

"He was covered in road grime, but dressed very nicely. He was well groomed."

"So, you deduced that he had gotten dirty that day?"

"Yes. And the red dust, mixed with the deeper browns, told me that he traveled on the road."

"Virden?"

"What town is within one day's distance?"

"Virden."

"Virden," he said.

"But he could have ridden from…" I began.

Anticipating my guess, Sir Locke said, "Not with that much road dust and dirt on him. And his shoes were caked. No, he definitely walked. Also, while his clothes were nice, they weren't extravagant. He wasn't lying about not having wealth."

"What about the ghost? You don't believe in ghosts, do you?" I said.

"Whether I believe in them, or not, that doesn't make them real, or not."

"But…"

"Latswin. It's important that we are willing to be wrong, otherwise, we may never find out the truth."

I thought it would be a good time to change the subject because, frankly, I wasn't fond of the idea of ghosts.

"I was thinking about your act," I said.

Sir Locke was, in many ways, an odd fellow. Even his choice of profession was a strange one.

My friend tried, but he just wasn't exceptional at entertaining. As a bard, you need to be able to perform in various ways - the normal ones being singing, joke-telling, storytelling, and perhaps dancing. Sir Locke excelled at none of these.

"Perhaps you could use your talents in deductive reasoning to entertain?" I tried.

"You mean like guessing people's weight, like in a carnival sideshow?" I couldn't hear any malice or anger in his voice, but I decided to tread softly nonetheless.

"More like where they had been, like you did with young Bavo?"

"Those are simple deductions, nothing to brag about. No, the real magic is in finding the truth behind those deductions. Like in this case."

"You mean finding out why he came to us? That's easy, your reputation is growing," I said.

"Yes, and I have you to thank for that. Those silly stories you keep writing, no doubt."

I knew my good friend pretty well, better than most. I knew that he wasn't actually thanking me at all.

"Well, look at the interesting cases it brings your way," I said.

"You make a good point. I apologize. Thank you."

I smiled. "You're very welcome."

We walked on in silence, again, for a short while.

"You know you shouldn't hold your past experiences against young Bavo, right?" Sir Locke said.

"What do you mean?" I asked.

"You shouldn't judge him by the actions of others."

"You mean Filmore Barrols, don't you?" I asked.

Sir Locke didn't answer, which was one of the clearest answers he had ever given me to one of my questions.

After another period of silence, I decided to try another question.

"So, what is the truth we're seeking?"

Now Sir Locke smiled. His patience was one of his greatest talents.

After a few minutes, when he saw that I still had no clue, he explained. "Honestly Latswin, I think it's actually quite obvious. We need to find out why a ghost is haunting the house."

We reached Virden at dusk.

"Should we go over to the Underfoot's?" Sir Locke asked.

"No, let's wait for the morning. If there really is a ghost, I'd much rather meet it in the light of day," I said.

Sir Locke smiled at this. And I realized he was teasing me. He had no intention of going straight to the Underfoot's. Not because of the ghost, but because it was late at night and he didn't want to be rude.

We found rooms at the Red Wolf Inn. The entertainment wasn't anything near what the Kenku had provided back in Little Thoracia, so Sir Locke actually paid attention to my queries this time.

"So, what do we do first?" I asked.

"Dinner I would think," he said. And as I'm always ready to eat, I readily agreed.

Dinner was acceptable. We had the house special, a mash of potatoes, mutton, and some unidentified vegetable.

"What do you think?" Sir Locke asked me.

"It's okay. Not as good as at the tavern, or my mom's, but not bad."

"I meant the case," he said.

"Oh. I think we should visit with the clients, and see if we can figure out what's going on," I said.

"Sounds reasonable."

"And the ghost?" I asked.

"We'll see," Sir Locke said.

"That's what I'm afraid of."

But the next morning we didn't start with the Underfoot twins. Their neighbor, Haryk Petinore, saw us coming, and was out in the road when we reached his yard.

"Are you Sir Locke, the gnome?" He was a well-dressed elf. I admit freely that I was fascinated. I had never seen an elf. They had not been common in the Empire for over fifty years. I didn't see any at the Autumn Gladiatorial Games, and none on our meager travels thus far. I had always heard about how elegant elves were. And this one seemed to match the reputation. He wore long flowing robes with a lot of shiny materials. Maybe even gold or silver woven into the cloth.

"Yes, I am," Sir Locke said.

"I'm so very honored to meet you." He was a good foot and a half taller than Locke, but you could tell he was in awe. He held out his hand and Locke shook it.

"I'm Haryk Petinore, the Underfoot's neighbor. It was my idea for them to seek your help, although I admit, I didn't think you'd actually come!"

"Why not?" I asked. Haryk turned to me with a look of surprise. He hadn't noticed me at all, or perhaps he didn't think I could speak.

"Oh, I'm so sorry. You must be the biographer, Latswin, right?"

"I'm a cleric, and Sir Locke's friend," I said.

"Oh, you're much more than that!" He said. "I've read your account of Sir Locke's first case, Cranks and Pranks." He grabbed my hand and shook it vigorously.

"I'd be so honored if you both would join me for lunch today. I don't think the twins will be able to provide you with much." As he said this, he turned and looked first at the humble little home ahead of us and then at his own luxurious house. Actually, it was a mansion. I had never seen such a large estate.

"I don't think…" Sir Locke began, but I cut him off quickly.

"Definitely. We'll be there. Noon, I presume?" It was all well and good that Sir Locke wanted to spend time with halflings and ghosts, but I wasn't going to miss the chance to dine with a real live elf, in his mansion!

"Noon it is. We can talk then. I won't hold you from your mission any longer," the elf said.

"Thank you…" I said. I wasn't sure how to address an elf. Were they all "highness" or something else?

"Haryk is fine," he said. "I think we'll soon be fast friends. If you need a place to spend the night before you head back, I have more than enough room." He turned and headed back down his long walkway to his front door.

"Are you coming Latswin?" Sir Locke called. He was already a good thirty paces away, walking briskly.

"Yes. Of course," I said and ran to catch up.

When we reached the front steps of the Underfoot's home, the door swung open and a couple came rushing out. They looked back over their shoulders once, and then hurried across the lawn. They were in the street before Sir Locke or I could stop them.

When we turned back to the doorway, a young halfling female was standing there. I jumped a little.

"I'm sorry. I didn't mean to frighten you," she said. She seemed very sad for someone so young.

"You must be the detective my brother hired? Sir Locke, is it? And you would be Mr. Gilshire, the cleric?" She offered her hand much as her neighbor had. Her hand was a lot smaller, but just as soft and gentle.

"Yes, but please, call me Latswin," I said.

"Thank you. And I'm Fara. Fara Underfoot."

"Two more potential buyers scared off?" Sir Locke asked.

"Yes, I'm *afraid* so." She giggled at her own use of "afraid." But I thought it was more of a nervous laugh, or an embarrassed one.

"The ghost?" Sir Locke asked.

"That's what they all say. I think it's just some rumor someone started, to keep us from selling the house," she said.

"You haven't seen this ghost?" I asked.

She looked at me apologetically.

"I'm sorry, I can't say I ever have. Bavo hasn't either. It never appears when we're around."

"So why don't you just stay with the buyers the whole time?" I asked.

"People want to look around without you there. They think if we're always with them, we don't trust them, or that we don't want them to find something that's wrong." She smiled at this. "And by what they say, there is."

"Very interesting," Sir Locke said. He was rubbing his chin. I had never seen him so engrossed in a case, and one that hadn't even started yet. "Can you please show us the house?"

"Of course."

She led us into the house. The house was well made. Each door a good heavy oak. We passed into the house after knocking the mud and grime off our shoes in the small entry space for outer clothing.

We passed through another door.

"This is the main room. There's a kitchen and a work room in the back. And a study off to the right. There are three bedrooms upstairs.

Sir Locke moved through the room with his customary disinterest. He never seemed to be studying anything but I knew he saw everything.

"What would you like to see first?"

"Where was your father's body found?" Sir Locke asked.

"We weren't here. We were told he was in the back room. It has a door to the back yard where they say the thief broke in," she explained.

The back room was used for storage; mostly gardening tools, another mat for wiping your feet, hooks for outer garments, and a workbench.

"My father loved gardening. It was his one guilty pleasure."

"Guilty?" I asked

"We didn't have any money. We lived very frugally and this was the only thing he spent money on."

I looked through the tools. All were well used, most looked second-hand. Nothing looked new.

Sir Locke bent down and rubbed his hand across the wood floor. He took out his dagger and scraped dirt from between the floorboards.   Fara watched him, probably afraid to say anything.

"His body was found here?" Sir Locke said pointing at the center of the floor.

"Yes, that's what we were told."

"And your brother said the neighbor found him?"

"Yes, Master Petinore."

Sir Locke walked over to the door and examined the lock. Then he opened it and walked into the back yard. It was recently tilled, the ground turned over across the entire 900 square foot area. It was a perfect square, 30 feet by 30 feet. The dark soil looked very rich. I couldn't help but think that Locke's mother would love this garden plot. She'd have planted a wide variety of flowers and plants in neat rows.

Sir Locke squatted down and picked up some soil. He rubbed it between his fingers.   Then he smelled it. Finally, he grabbed a larger handful and sifted it between his fingers. There were three small bulbs left in his palm. He let them drop back to the ground.

He came back in, again cleaning his shoes at the doorway first. He went over to the bench where I had inspected the tools, and reached up to a shelf.   He brought down a small slatted box. It was about a third full of Moon Lily bulbs. He looked them over carefully.

When he was done examining the room, he turned to our hostess.

"Please continue."

Without the slightest hint of impatience, she led us to the kitchen. It was directly across from the back room. This was a much quicker inspection. I thought he would look in the cabinets and pots, perhaps open the flour jar and empty the contents looking for a clue of some kind, but he barely paused. We moved on to the study.

"Was this where your father spent most of his time?" I asked. I wanted to feel useful. Many times, with Sir Locke, I felt like a fifth wheel on a cart. No real use unless one of the better wheels became damaged.

"You might think so," she said. The room had a fireplace, a table, a comfortable looking chair, a rug made from some type of animal hide, a collection of books on the mantle, and two large tapestries. "But I would say his favorite room in the house was the back room, and his favorite place to spend time was in the backyard. He loved gardening."

"How often did he rotate his flowers and plants?" Sir Locke asked. It always gave me a little surprise when he would ask a question on point, when I was sure he wasn't paying any attention.

"A few times a year. Looked like he was about to plant a new crop when, when he was killed," she said.

"These tapestries are of you and Bavo, age five or so?" Sir Locke asked.

They were nice tapestries, hung on the same wall, with a good three feet between them. There was a long wooden rod holding them, with two hooks each. They showed each child in a wooded scene, playing, or singing, or laughing. They were very joyous works.

"Yes. You might think they were expensive," she looked a little guilty, "but they weren't. My mother actually made them. She was very artistic."

She rubbed her hand over the material. "She may have been able to make a living making them, but she died soon afterward from an illness. These are our last keepsakes."

Sir Locke thoroughly inspected the room, checking each of the eight books on the mantle, looking behind the tapestries, going through the desk drawers. When he was done, we toured the upstairs. His inspection there was very quick. I thought he would check under the beds or in closets, but he breezed through each of the rooms in a few seconds. Within an hour of our arrival, we were back in the main room.

"I'd like to meet the ghost now," Sir Locke said as if he were asking for an audience with the owner of the house.

Fara looked a little worried. I could understand her fear. Everyone else who had seen the ghost had left in a hurry and hadn't come back.

"Don't worry. We won't be leaving," Sir Locke said, with more confidence than I felt.

"But it never appears while Bavo, or I, are in the room."

"Where is Master Bavo?" Sir Locke asked.

"He's in town getting us food for lunch. We have very little, and nothing appropriate for guests. He should be back shortly."

"That's fine. Would you please step outside and wait for his return? And stay there until we come out?" Sir Locke asked.

"I guess. But we don't usually leave the house"

"I understand. But would you do it for me?" Sir Locke asked.

"Of course." She looked around the room one more time, making sure she hadn't forgotten anything, and then went out the front.

After I was sure we were alone, I asked Sir Locke, "Why didn't you search the house for the inheritance?"

"My dear Latswin, why waste time? The thief already searched thoroughly. I was only looking for things he would have missed."

"I see," I said, not seeing at all.

I asked the second, more pressing question I had on my mind. "So, we *want* to see the ghost?"

"Of course!" Sir Locke said.

"But we're not buying the house…so perhaps it won't appear," I hoped.

"Nonsense. It wants to be seen and heard."

"So why not appear to his children?" I asked.

"I have a guess, but I'd rather not say, until I know more."

"And why does it want to be seen and heard? What does it want?" I hoped talking would keep it away. Or perhaps it was just a nasty rumor like Fara said.

"Ultimately it wants peace, or at least that's what I've read. But how it gains that peace, is part of the mystery." His eyes danced with excitement. "This case has more questions than any case we've encountered so far."

It seemed he really wanted to see this ghost. I, on the other hand, wasn't so sure that it was a good idea.

"So, what do we do? How do we get the ghost to come out?" I asked, despite myself.

"I assume we do what we have to do most times…wait."

We didn't have to wait long.

As you know by now, I'm not the most creative writer in the world. I try to be factual and clear, not adding a lot of fluff. Partly, because it's how I learned to write, becoming a cleric, and partly because Sir Locke demands it. But this time, I wish I had the talent to better describe what we saw.

At first, it was like a wisp of smoke. And then the smoke grew, became larger. It also seemed to become more solid. It came from the study, and circled the room twice. When we didn't run (the truth is, I would have definitely run, but my feet wouldn't move), it stopped in front of Sir Locke. He didn't seem afraid at all.

"I'm here to help," Sir Locke said. The ghost became a little more solid. You could tell it was a male, a halfling, but not much else. The features were distorted.

While I was very sure it couldn't feel pain, it seemed to be hurting the whole time.

It couldn't actually talk. It had an expression, if you can call it that. It looked as if it was perpetually screaming. And then I could hear it, but I knew it wasn't out loud, it was in my head. I could hear it screaming in my head. No wonder everyone ran from it. Even so, I couldn't help but feel sorry for it, even through my fear.

Sir Locke didn't waiver.

"I'm here to help. What do you want?"

Its expression changed for a moment. It just hung there in the air and then it circled the room again and headed down the hall.

"Hurry Latswin!" Sir Locke yelled as he ran after the specter.

It went through the door to the study, obviously leading us.

As we entered the room, it let out a scream, but I am sure it was only audible in our minds. It flew around the room once, and then plunged into the stone wall, between the tapestries. Both tapestries rippled from the current it generated.

It was gone.

"Well, that wasn't very helpful," I said.

"Actually, he told us all we needed to know," Sir Locke said.

"He? So, you think it's their father?"

"Yes, and we should be able to help him find peace."

"So, what now?" I asked.

"Let's go get lunch at the neighbor's." I was so happy to hear this, I didn't ask any more questions. I was really hungry (fear makes me hungrier than usual), and I was looking forward to seeing the elf again. And, I wanted to see his mansion too.

When we left the house, we saw that Bavo had returned. He had a small hand cart with groceries on it.

"So?" Bavo asked. There was a lot in that simple, one-word question.

"I'd like to eat lunch first," Sir Locke said.

The twins seemed a little taken back. They clearly had a lot of questions, but were too polite to argue.

"Of course. But it will take an hour or so to prepare it," Fara said.

"That should work out fine. We were invited to your neighbor's for lunch, and I'd like to visit him," Sir Locke said.

"So, second lunch it is!" Bavo said.

"That sounds good," I said. One thing I can say I like about halflings, is their concept of meal times. And, these twins were starting to make me feel that I may have been a little hasty in deciding all halflings were mean, and selfish creatures.

"Can I beg a favor from you?" Sir Locke asked.

"Of course," Bavo said. Sir Locke took him aside and gave him some instructions.

"Yes sir, right after I take the groceries to the kitchen for Fara."

Haryk Petinore answered the door himself. He had changed clothes, wearing a splendid ensemble, lots of purples and blues. There was a lavish spread set out on a long table in the dining room.

"I was hoping you'd come," Haryk said.

I wanted to say, 'I wouldn't miss it.' But all that came out was, "Uh huh."

"Thank you, master Petinore," Sir Locke said.

"Haryk, please."

"Haryk." Sir Locke said.

Petinore beamed.

After an extensive tour of the mansion, we sat down to a very nice meal. Haryk asked a lot of questions, wanting to know about Sir Locke's methods, and our previous cases. I was flattered that he had read my account of our first case. I normally want to focus on my food, but I didn't want to be rude. I knew lunch would have to wait, since Sir Locke rarely talked about himself.

To my surprise, Sir Locke started answering Haryk's questions.

I was very happy to dig into the food and listen to their conversation. The spread was impressive. Everything was extremely fresh, as if it had just been bought at market. It smelled terrific.

Sir Locke shared the story of the death of Tyann Rit, the Gladiatorial Champion, and then how he was knighted. He was very humble in his account, making it sound like it was all dumb luck.

Haryk ate while Sir Locke entertained. Not a legendary bardic performance, but my good friend did a fine job. Where most bards shine with a crowd, Sir Locke was better in a more private setting.

I had finished my plate and was taking a sip of mead, when Sir Locke slid his plate in front of me. He hadn't touched it. He kept talking, and I worked through his food.

"Amazing," Haryk said as he finished his meal. "Simply amazing."

Then it was Sir Locke's turn to ask, and Haryk's to answer.

"I noticed you have a beautiful collection of paintings," Sir Locke started.

"Thank you," Haryk said.

"They all seem to be the same artist?" Sir Locke asked.

"Yes, they are original pieces by Sicily Underfoot, the twin's mom," he said.

"I thought the style was familiar. I saw two tapestries she made in the Underfoot's study," Sir Locke said.

"Yes. She had a bright future. She was definitely an up and coming artist. It was very sad when she died."

"Did you get all of the pieces after she died?" Sir Locke asked.

"Yes, I wanted to help out the family, so I bought all of the works Polo would sell," Haryk said, and then as if he couldn't help himself he added, "at a good price too."

In the silence that followed he seemed to think better of it and added, "A fair price of course."

Sir Locke nodded.

"What can you tell me about your neighbor, Mr. Underfoot?" Sir Locke asked.

"Not much to tell…Polo was nice enough. He loved gardening."

"But he was pretty wealthy, wasn't he? The twins say he always promised them an inheritance?" Sir Locke asked.

I was surprised. I wasn't used to Sir Locke asking questions that he could deduce the answers to.

"No, he only owned that small house. He barely had enough money to buy food and clothes for his children. After his wife passed, he worked every day, and most nights, just to keep them going. I offered to help, but he was too proud for handouts."

"If I needed some help, how much interest would you charge?" Sir Locke asked, sounding every bit like a man needing financial aid.

"For you? I could manage it at ten percent. Did you need a loan?"

"No, thank you. Just wondered, in case, for the future."

"I offered Polo the same. But he was very prideful for such a poor man. Have you ever noticed that about the poor?"

"You're very observant," Sir Locke said, with a slight nod. That's when I realized he was interrogating Haryk. "But I'm curious, if he was always working, and they never had anything nice, what was he spending the money on?" Sir Locke asked innocently.

"Perhaps he was in debt?"

"Hmm. From what? He didn't have anything of value." Sir Locke seemed truly puzzled. What a great bard he was becoming.

"Probably the house. He kept saying the inheritance was *in* the house." Haryk said.

"I assumed his family had built it. It seems very rustic," Sir Locke said.

"You may be right. Perhaps he gambled away his earnings? Some people have troubles with gambling or drinking," Haryk said.

"Ah! But was he that type? He seemed to have been pretty down-to-earth. Like his love of gardening," Sir Locke said.

If you didn't know Sir Locke as well as I did, you would think he was totally captivated by Haryk's thoughts on the subject.

"Perhaps not. He didn't go out much," Haryk said.

"Well, if he worked as hard as you say, and didn't spend the earnings on frivolous things, what do you think he did with the money?" Sir Locke sounded totally puzzled.

"What do you mean by frivolous?" Haryk asked, a little defensively. I wondered if Sir Locke had gone too far.

"I mean he didn't have anything except the bare basics in his house. All of his tools looked old and well-used. His children say he had only one set of clothes, and those were patched and then re-patched. They said his shoes had been repaired at least three times," Sir Locke said.

"I see. Yes, he barely spent anything on even the essentials." Haryk said, once again becoming comfortable in Sir Locke's ignorance.

"But there was his garden," Sir Locke said.

"That's true. He had new flowers and plants every month!" Haryk said happily. "That must be it. We all have our flaws."

"So, you didn't believe him, that he had an inheritance for his children?" Sir Locke asked.

"No, you can believe me. He didn't. He had been talking about creating an inheritance ever since his wife died. And if he actually had one, I'd know."

"Sad," I said.

I didn't really mean to join in, but I couldn't help it. I was looking at the desserts, trying to pick one to try (there were five different kinds), and I was a little depressed that proper manners meant I had to pick only one.

"Yes, very sad," Haryk said. But he wasn't talking about the desserts.

We sat in silence a little while. A servant came in and started clearing the table. I grabbed a second dessert before it was taken away, and placed it in front of my friend.

As coffee was being served, Sir Locke broke the silence.

"I know it might be asking a lot, but could you show me where you found Mr. Underfoot's body?"

"Definitely," Haryk said. "Anything I can do to help. Do you have any idea how to find the thief?"

"No luck yet, so I'm hoping you'll remember something that might help," Sir Locke said. I almost smiled.

"Now?" Haryk asked. He seemed to enjoy being the center of Sir Locke's attention.

"No. No rush. Let's have our coffee first," Sir Locke said.

Was this my friend? Talking about 'luck?' And taking time for coffee, before working a case? I had seen his methods, but this was definitely new. If I didn't know better, I'd be worried that the ghost had possessed my friend.

"Locke?" I whispered. Sir Locke just smiled. This made me even more suspicious. When he slid his dessert over to me, I finally relaxed. This, at last, was normal behavior.

About thirty minutes later, all three of us were headed over to the Underfoot's. Haryk led us around the back of the house.

"You said you found him in the back room, right?" Sir Locke asked, still with an air of innocence.

"Yes. I had seen him gardening earlier in the day, so I was coming over to visit."

"Was the garden dug up like this?" We walked through the minefield of holes to the back door.

"Yes. He was digging up the yard in the morning. I guess he was turning it over for his next crop."

"Do you garden?"

Haryk laughed, and Sir Locke laughed along with him.

"No, it's not my thing," Haryk said.

"So, you don't know what these things are?" Sir Locke knelt down and picked up a handful of bulbs.

"I'm guessing seeds?"

"No. I think they're bulbs. Moon Lilly bulbs to be precise." Sir Locke said. I knew that Locke knew more about flora and fauna than most gardeners. His mother loved gardening and was a perennial award winner for her flowers.

Haryk figured Sir Locke was showing off. It was normal for Haryk. He had shown off his clothes, his home, his servants, and the meal. Now it was Sir Locke's turn to show off. It's the way it was done. I'm sure Haryk thought nothing more of it.

"So please tell me what happened," Sir Locke said.

"I suspect that a vagrant traveling through saw Polo working in his garden, and figured he was an easy mark." Haryk said.

"Hmm. Alright." Sir Locke seemed to think this over. "But why would this traveling thief think Mr. Underfoot had anything worth stealing?" Sir Locke sounded fascinated by Haryk's abilities of deduction.

"I don't know. Maybe he figured everyone had something worth stealing. I mean he *was* a homeowner," Haryk said.

"Wasn't Mr. Underfoot poorly dressed?" Sir Locke asked.

"He wasn't elegantly dressed, he was working in the garden," Haryk said.

"Right!" Sir Locke seemed excited by Haryk's observation. "So, he looked more like a gardener than the owner of the house?"

"True…" Haryk said.

Sir Locke looked perplexed by this.

"Maybe the thief just wanted to rob the house?" Haryk offered.

"But why attack the gardener? Why not just sneak into the house while it was empty?" Sir Locke asked.

"Perhaps the front door was locked, and he was going to sneak in the back. And, then, Polo noticed him! Or he just thought it was easier to knock Polo out and then go in the open back door," Haryk rambled.

"Maybe! You're pretty good at this," Sir Locke said.

"It's elementary. You just have to know people." Haryk said.

Sir Locke nodded. "So, how do you think it happened?"

"Okay. Let's see. I've been thinking about this. I figure the vagrant was walking by, and saw Polo in the backyard. He figured he could overpower the gardener and ransack the house," Haryk said.

"But Mr. Underfoot didn't have anything of value in the house…" Sir Locke added.

"Right, but the vagrant wouldn't know that," Haryk continued.

"And, he comes into the house, surprising Mr. Underfoot. They fight," Sir Locke offered.

"No, no. The vagrant sneaks up behind him, and hits him over the head with a shovel," Haryk corrected.

"How do you know he didn't put up a fight? If the house was all he had, wouldn't he fight for it?" Sir Locke asked.

"Why would he fight? He knew there wasn't anything of value," Haryk said.

"Good point. But still wouldn't he be upset with a thief entering his house?" Sir Locke asked.

"No. You didn't know him. He would have probably offered him lunch and a bed for the night." The elf obviously thought this was a ridiculous idea, one that he would never have done.

"So, the vagrant never gave him a chance, he snuck up behind him and hit him with a shovel? Like this one?" Sir Locke picked up a heavy spade.

"Yeah that looks right."

"Was there a lot of blood?" Sir Locke asked.

Haryk thought about it. "No, not really."

"Was there an open wound? Perhaps the skin wasn't broken?" Sir Locke asked.

"No, there was a big ugly gash," Haryk said. "There was a lot of blood. I forgot because it was under his body. I didn't even notice it until after the constable came," Haryk said.

At that moment, Fara came into the back room.

"We thought we heard voices," Fara said.

Bavo came in right behind her, followed by the constable. He was a big man, even for a human. And he looked very formidable. I could see why Virden passed an ordinance requiring all buildings to meet minimum size requirements. If the house were a normal halfling-sized house, he would never fit inside.

"Hi, Sir Locke? Mr. Gilshire? I'm Constable Stalard." He shook our hands.

Haryk seemed happy to have a larger audience.

"Don't let us stop you, we're all happy that you've agreed to take on this case. Everyone liked Polo," the constable said.

"Well, that's great timing really. Mr. Petinore was just explaining that he found Mr. Underfoot here on the floor, dead. Is that right?" Sir Locke said.

"Yes. And, there was a lot of blood," Haryk said.

"Yes, we had a real hard time cleaning up the stain," Fara agreed.

"And you called the constable right away?" Sir Locke asked Haryk.

"I sent one of my servants to get him while I stayed with poor Polo," Haryk said.

"And when you arrived, Constable Stalard, was everything as you expected?" Sir Locke asked.

"What do you mean?" The constable asked.

"I mean, did everything seem like a thief, traveling through Virden, saw a man gardening, decided to rob the house, came in the back following Polo, and hit him over the head with a shovel, killing him?" Sir Locke recited.

The constable thought it over.

"Well, not exactly."

"How do you mean?" Sir Locke asked.

"Well, Mr. Underfoot was on his back. His arms were by his sides."

"Why is that not what you expected?" Sir Locke asked.

"Normally, when someone is hit really hard from behind, they fall forward. He should have been on his face."

Haryk offered an explanation, although the constable was speaking to Sir Locke. "Perhaps, he turned him over after hitting him, to see if he was alive? Maybe he didn't mean to kill him?"

"Hmmm. Anything else?" Sir Locke asked.

"If he did fall backward, it's rare that his arms would be by his side. His body would be a jumble, not so neat." The constable said. Sir Locke seemed impressed. I know he didn't normally hold much faith in law-keepers.

"If he checked to see if he was dead, he may have moved his arms too," Haryk said.

"Anything else?" Sir Locke asked, continuing to ignore Petinore.

The constable seemed happy to have someone actually listen to him, and perhaps, understand his reasoning. He thought hard.

"Like what Sir? What did I miss?" Constable Stalard asked.

"That's hard to say, as it was a long time ago. Think back. Tell me about his shoes," Sir Locke said.

"Shoes?"

"Yes. Were they muddy? He had been out working in the garden. Were they muddy on the bottom?" Sir Locke asked.

"Why, yes. They were caked with mud. But that wasn't unexpected," Constable Stalard said.

"And Fara, you cleaned the floor?" Sir Locke asked.

"Yes," she said.

"Was the blood only in this area?" Sir Locke pointed to the rug she had placed to hide the stain.

"No, there was a trail from the door to the spot," she said.

"So, we can surmise that he was attacked outside and dragged into the house!" The constable said.

"Quite right," Sir Locke said. "But what I don't understand is how a thief would have been able to sneak up on poor Mr. Underfoot, in broad daylight?"

This was one of his best performances I had ever seen.

"It wasn't daylight yet," Haryk said, caught up in the flow of conversation and a little annoyed that he was no longer the center of attention.

"It was night?" Sir Locke asked.

"No, just before dawn," Haryk said.

"Mr. Petinore, you told me you found Mr. Underfoot in the afternoon," the constable said.

"Yes, that's right," Haryk said.

"But…" the constable began, before Sir Locke cut him off.

"So, help me get this all straight, Mr. Pen…Haryk," Sir Locke said, looking very focused. "The body was here, face up, like this." Sir Locke actually laid down. "And where was his shovel?"

"Outside!" Mr. Petinore said, pushing to reestablish his position.

"And where was his bag of bulbs?" Sir Locke continued.

"There, on the table," Haryk said. He walked over, and pointed at a spot on the table.

"But, where did he drop the bag? Inside or outside?" Sir Locke said sitting up. He was giving Haryk all of his attention. As if they were the only two in the room.

"Outside. The thief must have brought it in and put it on the table," Haryk said.

"And Haryk, are those the same shoes you were wearing at the time?" Sir Locke said, looking at Haryk's shoes.

"No, they were bloody. I threw them away." Haryk said.

"Because of blood on the soles? That would have worn off over time. Seems a shame to waste a good pair of shoes," Sir Locke said.

"Yes, but the blood on the rest wouldn't come out."

"Oh, you mean the spatter on the toes?" Sir Locke asked without missing a beat.

"Yes, in the eyeholes, and laces too." Haryk said, not thinking.

"I see." Sir Locke said. "Is that enough, Constable Stalard?" Sir Locke asked.

"More than enough." The constable pulled a shank of rope from his large pockets and grabbed Haryk's wrists.

He yanked them back and behind Haryk, quickly tying them together.

"What? What are you doing?" Haryk asked.

"Arresting you, for the murder of Polo Underfoot. Thanks to Sir Locke the gnome," the constable said.

"What did he tell you? You're going to believe this stranger over me? I've lived here for 140 years!" Haryk said.

"Sir Locke didn't tell me anything, you did. You just confessed, although for the life of me, I don't know why you killed him. Such a nice little old man. He never hurt anyone. Hardest worker I ever met." The constable cinched up the knot tighter.

"Ow!" Haryk protested.

"Why'd he do it? Why'd he kill his neighbor? What could old, poor, Mr. Underfoot have that this rich dodger would want enough to kill him?" The constable seemed genuinely concerned. I happily admit that I had many more questions than that I wanted answered.

"I didn't…" Haryk tried.

The constable smacked the back of Haryk's head. "I've heard enough out of you. I'm asking Sir Locke."

"Why does anyone do something so awful? In this case, I would say it was a mix of greed and jealousy," Sir Locke said.

"Why in the world would he be jealous of our dad?" Fara asked.

"He believed your dad's stories about your inheritance," Sir Locke said.

"But why? Look at this house. My father had only one set of clothes. He had no money!" Bavo said.

"That's an incorrect deduction. Just because your father didn't spend money, didn't mean he was poor. Most times, looks are meant to deceive."

"So, the inheritance is real?" Fara asked.

"Haryk thought so," Sir Locke said.

"But why would he be jealous? He's already rich!" Bavo tried.

"Looks are meant to deceive," Sir Locke repeated.

They looked at each other and then at Haryk who was busy saying nothing.

"Constable Stalard, when you check, I'm sure you'll find that our good neighbor, Mr. Petinore, is heavily in debt." Sir Locke said.

"How can you know that? You've been in town less than a day," the constable asked.

"We ate lunch with Mr. Petinore," Sir Locke said.

The constable looked at him, waiting.

"I'm sorry. During lunch, the dish and silverware the staff used didn't match. If you hire temporary staff when you want to appear wealthy, they make mistakes. They don't know where all of the pots, pans, and dishes are," Sir Locke said.

"Temporary staff? That was enough to…" Constable Stalard started.

"Also, he had sold his original paintings. He bought them from Mr. Underfoot after his wife died, at a 'good price' and then resold them for a large profit. To keep up appearances, he paid some much less talented artist to replicate the pieces. The ones hanging in his home are poor imitations. He obviously doesn't know how to hold on to his money," Sir Locke said.

The constable nodded, actually understanding.

"And this jealousy led to him killing our father?" Bavo asked.

"Petinore undoubtedly believed your dad's stories of a great inheritance, he was planning to give to his children. He believed it enough that when he saw Polo out in the dark, burying something in his yard, that he thought he was burying his treasure. He snuck up behind him, as elves are very capable of doing, and hit him with Mr. Underfoot's own shovel," Sir Locke said.

Haryk didn't argue.

"Perhaps he didn't mean to kill him, only to rob him. But alas, our Mr. Petinore is not accomplished at anything except spending money," Sir Locke finished.

"So, he stole the inheritance?" I asked. I had been watching and listening to this fantastic story, and had to finally ask some questions.

"No, Latswin. If you notice, the yard is totally dug up."

"Wasn't that Mr. Underfoot planting?" I asked.

"No. The Moon Lilly bulbs were already planted. He only had a few more to go. Moon Lillies need to be planted before sunrise, and you'll find them discarded all around the yard. No, that was Mr. Petinore, desperately looking for the treasure."

"How about the house?" I asked.

"Ah. He searched the house also. First, he called the constable and reported the crime. His bringing the body inside did two things for him; first, it allowed him to search the yard. Anyone passing by would think it was either Mr. Underfoot gardening, or that his neighbor was helping him prepare the ground for the next crop."

Sir Locke picked up a few Moon Lilly bulbs and put them back in the bin.

"Secondly, it was his excuse for being in the house." Sir Locke looked at the constable. "I'll wager that he told you he had come to the back door and saw his body."

"Why yes, that's what he said. And that he had seen someone leaving the property," the constable said.

"But remember, he killed Mr. Underfoot before dawn, besides his own admittance of the time, we know it because Polo was still planting bulbs when he was killed. But he reported the crime later in the day," Sir Locke said. "And, after you removed the body, he spent the next week thoroughly ransacking the house. When he still failed to find anything, he sent word to Mr. Underfoot's children."

Fara and Bavo nodded their heads.

"So, the rich, elegantly dressed, handsome elf, was actually broke?" I asked, looking at the prisoner. "And the guy who had one set of clothes, no worldly possessions, and worked every day of his life was rich?" I found this all impossible to believe.

Sir Locke nodded.

"But he was so generous," I said, remembering our lunch.

"Not really. He offered to help the twins, if they paid interest. He gave us lunch, but that was to see what we had found out. He was checking to see that his story of a vagrant thief was holding up, and hoping that we would find clues to where the treasure was," Sir Locke explained.

"So, he wanted us to show up?" I asked.

"No, that was a mistake on his part. I'm sure if he's read your silly stories, he didn't *really* want us here. He was hoping the twins would give up and leave, so he could tear the house apart, literally. He couldn't do so without first taking possession." Sir Locke said.

"But he never offered to buy the house," Bavo said.

"No, that would be too obvious. He did send people to try and buy it for him though," Sir Locke said.

"All of the buyers were his?" Fara asked.

"I'm sure there were only a few, probably the first ones. You probably had a few potential buyers show up before you even made it known you wanted to sell it?" Sir Locke asked.

"Yes, that's true," Bavo said.

"So, what went wrong? His plan sounds perfect," the constable asked.

"Someone he didn't count on, messed up his plans," I said.

"Right you are Latswin, but not who you think. I'm not the reason his plans failed. It was Polo Underfoot that did him in," Sir Locke said. "Your father wouldn't let you sell this house. He was protecting your inheritance. It was the most important thing in his life, and that has kept his spirit here. He loved you both very much."

"Why didn't he give it to us before we left?" Fara asked.

"I don't know," Sir Locke said. That sounded very odd to my ears. I can't remember a time he didn't know the answer to a question.

"Would you venture a guess, please?" She asked.

I knew my good friend would not guess; he loathed guesswork.

"Please?" She repeated.

"I have nothing to support my assumptions. My guess is literally as good as yours. Or the Constable's. Or Latswin's," I took no affront to being included. The way I saw it, my good friend just paid me a large compliment. To think, my guess was as good as his!

"Please?" She asked again.

Locke looked down. I had never seen him like this before.

And then he surprised me once again. He actually answered the young halfling.

"I think it's because he had seen what wealth could do to people. He had watched his neighbor for years, your whole childhood, squander his wealth. Haryk Petinore bought things he couldn't afford; the finest of everything, caring only about appearances," Sir Locke said looking at Petinore.

Then he looked at the twins and I saw great sadness in his eyes.

"He also saw how you two were embarrassed by his simple life, his lack of finery. It hurt him that neither of you appreciated him, or what you had."

Fara began to sob. Bavo walked over and put his arms around her. He gave her a hug.

"Please, continue," Bavo said.

"He wanted you to appreciate what you had, what it takes to earn an honest living. He had scrimped and saved so you could live better than he did. You could have a better house, better clothes, better furniture, a better life. But he realized that if he just gave it to you, that it might do more harm than good."

Sir Locke looked at Haryk who was also sobbing.

"He undoubtedly planned to give you his gift, the inheritance, after you had learned the true value of hard work. He wanted you to be a better steward of the wealth he had built up for you. Better people than he saw in his neighbor."

"That's a pretty good guess," Bavo said. "I think you are spot on."

Everyone nodded, even Haryk.

Fara's tears were contagious. We were all wiping our faces.

In light of Locke's suppositions, I was sure no one would ask what they still all wanted to know. So, I asked.

"So where is the treasure?"

Sir Locke looked at the twins. They nodded in agreement.

"Let's go into the study." We all walked to the study, Sir Locke leading the way. The twins came next, then me, and finally the constable dragging Haryk along.

When we were all there, Sir Locke stood against the wall, between the two tapestries.

"These two tapestries were his prized possessions."

"How do you know that?" The constable asked.

"There is a healthy coat of dust on everything in the room, except these tapestries. He kept these very clean. Even the hooks."

The twins didn't move.

"Your father's ghost came into this room and exited right behind me," Sir Locke said.

Sir Locke moved over to the twins, and gently guided them toward the tapestries, each toward the one of themselves.

"I looked there," Haryk said.

Sir Locke ignored him.

"Could you both reach up and pull down the hook furthest away from each other?" There were two hooks with a dowel between them, holding the tapestry.

"I tried that," Haryk said.

"Yes, I thought you did. But Polo Underfoot was too smart for you. He set the mechanism to require his children to work together. Fara and Bavo, please pull down at the same time."

They looked at each other nervously, maybe a little scared. Not excited at all. Perhaps the gravity of the sacrifices their father made for them had finally set in.

With a slight nod, they both pulled down on their hooks, standing on their tiptoes. There was a soft 'click' sound and then a grinding. A set of bricks, between the tapestries, shifted a little and worked their way forward. Dust came out, and scraping sounds. Everyone looked at the bricks, in shock. Fara and Bavo pulled out the bricks together, tears flowing again. They carried the false bricks, and the hidden treasure box over to the table.

Polo Underfoot was more successful at saving, investing, and building an inheritance for his children than even Haryk had imagined. There was enough there that neither twin would have to work another day in their lives.

"That was amazing," the constable said.

Sir Locke looked at Haryk, smiled and said, "Elementary."

We spent the night in town, at the inn. We wanted to give the twins time alone. I, of course, had to get the rest of my questions answered.

"So, when did you know the neighbor was the culprit?" I asked.

"I wasn't sure until he slipped up in our interrogation."

"Over lunch?" I asked.

"No, that was the beginning. We ended at the Underfoot house, when he basically explained how he did it, the shoes were the frosting on the cake. He couldn't have gotten blood on the top of his shoes unless he was the killer. He had a lot of motive, although no one suspected it because no one else believed in the Underfoot treasure."

"Okay and how did you know where the treasure was or how to open it?" I asked.

"The ghost led us to the room. When the tapestries moved, I noticed they were the only well-kept items in the room. Like Haryk, I found the loose hooks. Unlike Haryk, I realized that the outer hooks were nine feet apart, so that they couldn't be moved at the same time, by one person. It would take two."

"Then how did Underfoot access it?" I asked. I figured he had to add to the chest from time to time.

"He actually didn't. Once he had saved enough, he put it there when he built it. He had investments all over town and the paperwork to prove it was in the chest."

"How rich are the twins now?" I asked.

"You know how wealthy you thought the elf was?"

"Yes, that much?" I asked.

Sir Locke smiled.

"More?" I asked.

"Much, much more," he said.

Before we left the next morning, the twins stopped by to thank us, and see us off.

"Thank you both for what you've done, for us, and for our father," Bavo said. He handed Sir Locke a small basket. It was full of Moon Lilly bulbs.

"Thank you very much," Sir Locke said. "My mother will love these."

"Fara and I thought you'd like them," Bavo said.

He also handed Sir Locke an envelope with a note for our fee. When they wouldn't let us refuse payment, Sir Locke decided he could put the funds to good use. He said he wanted to help the street urchins running around, by giving them a clear purpose. He also told me he planned to move out of his mother's house and take the small apartment above the baker's shop.

"So, do you think you'll be able to sell the house now?" I asked.

"I'm sure we could. I don't think father's ghost is there any longer." He looked a little depressed.

"Why didn't he ever show himself to us? I would have liked to say goodbye," Fara said.

"I'm sure he didn't look like your father, what we saw was pretty fearsome," Sir Locke said. "Our memories are our greatest treasure and he didn't want your memory of him tainted."

She nodded.

"Thank you again. You've changed our lives," She said.

We headed back to Little Thoracia with Sir Locke's goodies.

"So, now you are a life changer too!" I teased my friend.

"Not the way you think," He said.

"What do you mean?"

"They are giving most of their inheritance away, to help orphaned children," Sir Locke said.

"Really? I guess they really did change."

"Yes. The inheritance their father left them, what it meant to work hard and save, was worth a lot more than the money they found."

The End

Book Five

The Case of the False Detective

The Adventures of Sir Locke the gnome

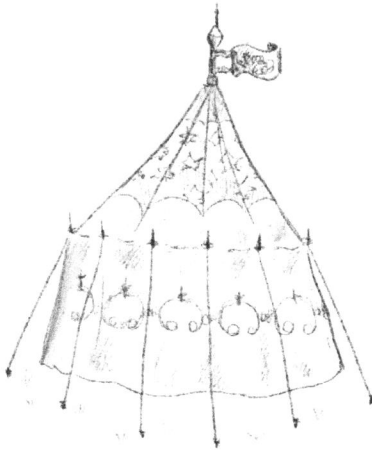

The Case of the False Detective

By Latswin Gilshire, Cleric

I don't mean to brag, but I feel like I had something to do with spreading the news about my best friend's amazing abilities as a detective. Granted, I had only written one story at this time, but still, it attracted a lot of attention; some welcome and some not so much.

We had recently returned from an adventure in Virden, a neighboring village, when I was approached about that first story, "A Case of Pranks and Cranks." We were seated at our usual table in The Inn (there being only one in Little Thoracia, there was no need for a name beyond, "The Inn"). I was working on my first service of mutton and beans. A gentleman, a human not much taller than Sir Locke, asked if he could speak with us.

"Do you mind if I join you?"

"After such a long journey? The least we can do is offer you a drink and a chair," Sir Locke said.

The man smiled broadly at this. "You must be Sir Locke the Gnome."

"Your deductive abilities are excellent," Sir Locke said with only the hint of a smile.

"Ha! Not at all. I have none of the special talents you have. I simply asked at the bar." He sat down. While he was only about a foot and a half taller than Sir Locke, he seemed to fill the room. In a gnome village, he was pretty tall, but he seemed wider than he was tall, which of course wasn't possible.

Sir Locke motioned for our waitress to bring more ale.

"Most deductions are actually just gathered information masquerading as conclusions," Sir Locke said.

"I like that! You should include that in your next story Mr. Gilshire," the man said, slapping me on the back. I dropped my fork and the food on it went across the table and onto the floor. I didn't bother to look after it. Anything that hit the floor would be snatched up by the cleaning crew (three dogs that lived at The Inn). Usually, they took care of accidents before you could count to five.

This big fellow was a very jovial human indeed. Most humans I'd encountered to that point were either very serious or aloof. This one was different.

I had learned my lesson in Virden about thinking everyone who looked alike were the same. I now realized that every person; halfling, elf, gnome, human, or dwarf was unique in themselves and although they may share observable traits, there was no way to determine the character of a person from their race. Or from their profession, or their gender. It had become much harder to decide who I liked.

"You have us at a disadvantage," Sir Locke said. "All I know about you is that you've traveled from Grimstone to offer my friend here, Latswin, a lucrative proposition. Would you mind sharing your name?"

"G. Newnes Le'Strand, esquire, at your service." He bowed his head to Sir Locke and then laughed heartily. He wiped a tear from each of his eyes. "You definitely don't disappoint! I didn't believe you were real until just now."

"Of course he's real. What did you think he was, an illusion?" I asked. While I may not judge all humans by the ones I have met, I still found it very hard to understand them.

G. Newnes Le'Strand laughed again, and slapped me on my back once again. I was ready this time and avoided losing any food.

"And you!" he said, looking me up and down. "You're much funnier in person than in your stories. You need to show your quick wit more in your writings. You don't do yourself justice." He laughed some more. "I meant; I wondered if Sir Locke the Gnome was just a character you invented. Who would believe that he was real? I mean, wow!"

I moved my chair around the table so I was next to Sir Locke, facing our visitor. My back was getting sore.

"How'd you know where I was from? Or why I'm here?" G. Newnes asked.

"This is a very small town. There's not much that doesn't get around," Sir Locke said.

This gave the man pause. He actually seemed to be thinking about it.

I looked at my friend wondering what he was up to. Usually he didn't hesitate to show off how he came to his amazing conclusions. But this time he was playing coy.

"Perhaps," G. Newnes said, to himself mostly.

I took another bite of my food. The ale arrived at the table and Sir Locke paid for the tankard. The waitress poured our new friend a large mug and topped off ours. When she left, G. Newnes looked at Sir Locke carefully.

"But you are real."

"Definitely," Sir Locke agreed.

"And the things Mr. Gilshire wrote about in his story, they're true, are they not?" G. Newnes asked.

"He tends to embellish a bit," Sir Locke said.

I tried to protest but the mutton wasn't chewed enough to allow me to argue. I started to raise my hand but Sir Locke pushed my hand back down, patting it.

"So, the story is fiction?" G. Newnes asked, pulling a copy of the Grimstone Gazette from his jacket pocket. It was rolled up, but I could see the imprint of the Grimstone Publishing House clearly on the left back corner. I smiled. My friend noticed things that I only saw when they were put in front of my face.

"Does it matter? In either case, you will be dealing with the author, not the subject of the story." It was dawning on me that Sir Locke and G. Newnes were in the middle of some kind of negotiation.

"Yes, that seems to be correct." G. Newnes turned his chair toward me, making a loud commotion as his chair scraped along the floor. He looked at me, carefully, as if he hadn't just slapped me on the back, twice. As if he was just meeting me for the first time.

"Mr. Latswin Gilshire, I represent the Grimstone Publishing House. The biggest publisher in the Empire. My name is G. Newnes Le'Strand, but I would be honored if you would refer to me as George." He stood up and reached out his hand.

I looked at Sir Locke and he nodded. I stood up and took the man's hand and shook. I sat back down and picked up my fork.

"Hmph," Sir Locke cleared his throat.

I looked up and G. Newnes was still standing.

"Oh. Please, join us," I said.

He sat back down, slapped the table hard enough to make my plate jump, and gave out another hardy laugh. He took a long drag on his mug.

I picked up my mug with my free hand, no reason to put down a perfectly good fork, eating heartily required talent. I took a sip of my ale, glad that he hadn't spilled any of our drinks.

"Mr. Gilshire, may I call you Latswin?"

"Sure, I don't see why not," I said.

"Excellent!   Latswin, I'm here to offer you a proposition.   We, the Grimstone Publishing House, would like to have exclusive rights to printing your stories about Sir Locke the Gnome." G. Newnes didn't look at Sir Locke once. He was totally focused on me. I have to admit this made me a little nervous.

"We're offering a nice stipend for your work.   We would like you to write one per month."

I sat in shock. I took another sip of ale to hide my inability to say anything intelligent.

"And how much do you intend to pay Mr. Gilshire for the first story you printed, without permission?" Sir Locke asked.

"Of course, the full fee. Here, here it is. Even if you don't want to go into contract with us, we are happy to pay you for the use of your first story." He pulled out a large satchel and shook out 10 gold into the palm of his large hand. He made two stacks of 5 gold pieces in front of me. I'll admit, I was speechless. I never thought my little story would actually be worth anything, much less be a way of earning more.

"And if Mr. Gilshire doesn't want to write any more stories?" Sir Locke asked. At this G. Newnes smiled broadly.

"I don't need to be a detective to know that's unlikely. Latswin, you have talent. And I've never met a talented person that would willingly hide his talent. We just want to be the ones to publish what you write. I'm willing to bet that you've already written another story. Am I wrong?" G. Newnes asked.

I didn't want to look at my friend. I had indeed written a story about Sir Locke's second case and had notes on two more.

"You are correct," Sir Locke said.

I looked at Sir Locke.

He just smiled at me.

"But, I believe you're low-balling my friend. You wouldn't have traveled all the way from Grimstone, for stories only worth 10 gold pieces. I'd wager you are ready to pay twice that to guarantee that you have exclusive rights," Sir Locke said.

"Are you a detective or a thief?" G. Newnes said and then laughed again. This time louder than before. "I give, I give. No more bartering. Latswin, I'm authorized to offer you up to 25 gold pieces for each story, if you can produce them monthly for our main periodical. We'll pay you for 10 months and then we can revisit the contract. If it's as popular as we expect, we will have made a good investment. If it's less, we'll likely end the contract."

"And if it's more?" Sir Locke asked. I was still speechless.

"Then we can revisit the stipend. We're a fair house. We want to save where we can, but we won't cheat you," G. Newnes said. I knew that he would have been happy to pay me only a fifth of what he was authorized to, but this wasn't cheating - in his perspective. That was just good business.

With more of a flourish than I thought his girth would allow, he produced a rolled parchment from an inner pocket. He held it out for me.

Sir Locke took it, my hands were full, with my mug of ale and my fork, so I was grateful for his assistance.

"Read it over. I'll come back tomorrow for your decision," George said.

"And the payment for the first story?" Sir Locke asked.

"Keep that no matter what you decide."

Sir Locke looked at him sternly.

"Oh, yes. Of course." G. Newnes said, taking out his satchel again. He once again counted out gold coins. This time three stacks of five each. He pushed these three over next to the other two.

He stood up and held out his hand again to me.

"We hope you decide to work with us. It was a pleasure to meet you Mr. Latswin Gilshire." I stood up and realized the fork was still in my hand. I dropped it onto my plate, wiped my hand on my trousers, and shook his hand.

He nodded to Sir Locke and left.

"Breath Latswin," Sir Locke said.

I sat down and let out a large sigh. I looked at the neat pile of gold coins in front of me.

"I'm a cleric, not a writer," I finally said.

"Can't you be both?" Sir Locke asked.

"I don't know. I'm not that good," I said.

"The evidence says differently."

"How'd you know he was from Grimstone? Or that he wanted to pay me for my stories? Or…"

Sir Locke held up his hand.

"I didn't need to deduce anything. Your cousin, Gobnac sent me a letter to let me know Mr. Le'Strand would come calling. He also told me how much you should ask for. You know I don't have a head for business."

My friend was not being humble. He didn't have the slightest interest in business, negotiations, or money. He saw it only as a means to gathering information, testing his theories, and obtaining tools that assisted him in his passion - solving mysteries. He was addicted to solving the unknown.

Of course, if he put his mind to it, he could be a great businessman. But he had no interest in it. I don't think he could have been great at two things. He had to pick.

That's part of what bothered me.

"Can I be a writer and a cleric? Won't I only be mediocre at both?" I asked.

"I'm a detective and a bard, why can't you be a cleric and a writer?" Sir Locke asked.

"But you're not a very good bard," I said.

Sir Locke laughed aloud. Not as loudly as our guest had, but it was a real, deep, laugh. I smiled and returned to my meal. I enjoyed making my friend laugh - he was always so serious.

"You know, as your doctor..." I chewed some more mutton. "..I wish I could prescribe laughter. If anyone ever needed to laugh more, it's you." I said. And immediately regretted it.

"Why do you think I hang around with you?" Sir Locke shot back.

"Because you needed someone to document your genius?" I offered, relieved.

"Or someone to keep me humble," he said.

We both started laughing and didn't stop until trouble walked into The Inn.

We had seen some really good bards already. Last month a visiting Kenku, Pluck, made music with her voice. Like the best Mocking Jay imaginable. She was special. Then of course there were all of Locke's classmates. And, well, Locke himself.

But the guy that walked through the door that night may have been the most unique we'd ever seen.

"Ladies and gentlemen! The time is nigh! Tomorrow you will have the distinct and rare opportunity to witness the here-to-fore unimaginable, the unbelievable, the fantastic brought to your doorstep."

He swept into The Inn, handing out flyers. He was a tall human, with a shiny bald head, a large hoop earring in his right ear lobe, and a flowing robe of many colors.

"The Empire's greatest carnival ever to grace the sands of Port Umbraah, the trees of the Duskhallow Forest, or the planes of the Great Grass Sea has arrived in the sister city of Thoracia, the true center of Gnome life."

I admit, I was impressed by his showmanship, but there was more.

"Now we don't expect you to believe our word for it. As with all true spectacular events in your life, there is forewarning. A hint. A clue."

At this my friend's demeanor noticeably changed. Most might not have noticed, but I had spent most of my life with my good friend. I knew when he was intrigued and this man's schtick was definitely getting Sir Locke's attention.

"Besides the hairless dwarf of Surtur's Forge, the dancing bears of Vulfstaag, and the winged woman of Thoracia, you will have the pleasure of experiencing, nay, of witnessing, the greatest detective in the known Empire."

At this Sir Locke leaned forward in his chair.

"And good people, you have the unique opportunity to see this detective at work, for I am he. Chaloner McCloundy, purveyor of deductive, and inductive, reasoning. You will be able to tell your children, and grandchildren, that you were among the first to see the extraordinary reasoning powers of the Great Chaloner!"

He waved his hand with a flourish and bowed deeply.

"Good sir..." he swept his hand to the right, opening it palm up, toward Rumbar the barber. "No reason to doubt." Rumbar stopped whispering to his companion. "And yes, you are correct, you won't see me in your shop any time soon." He rubbed his shiny smooth head.

Everyone clapped.

"How'd he know he was the barber?" I asked Sir Locke.

"Shhh, Latswin, the show has only just begun," Sir Locke said.

There was a commotion. Three young gnomes, all friends, shoved a fourth out into the middle of the floor. They laughed heartily. "Tell his fortune!" One of them shouted.

"Alas, my good fellows, I don't tell fortunes. But I will deduce some facts about this young gnome if you like."

There were cheers of encouragement, and more than just the young gnome's friends were laughing.

"Are you sure?" the Bard asked as he grabbed the young gnome's hand. He shook it firmly, while gripping his shoulder with his other hand. "I don't think he wants me to tell his secret, or ruin the surprise."

His friends laughed harder, but the young gnome seemed very scared. "No, no, please."

"Why? Is she here?" The Great Chaloner asked.

"No, but..."

"Ah. Of course. Perhaps you can bring her to the carnival tomorrow? We can arrange something special if you like." He whispered something in the gnome's ear. The gnome nodded his head and grabbed Chaloner's hand with both of his. He shook it vigorously.

"Thank you. Thank you." He looked at his friends angrily and then headed out the exit. His friends ran after him.

"What was that all about?" I asked Sir Locke.

"He's going to propose to his girlfriend tomorrow at the show." Sir Locke said, calmly, without any hesitation.

"I'd much rather have a willing participant than someone who is forced into it. Who would like me to tell them about themselves? How about you?" Chaloner said, gesturing his open palm, with his arm fully extended, directly at me.

I looked at Sir Locke. He nodded to me.

"Okay. I have nothing to hide," I said, and stood up.

He shook my hand as he had the young gnome's, and like with the young gnome he put his large (humans were all pretty large compared to gnomes) hand on my right shoulder. He gave it a firm, but gentle squeeze.

"Thank you. I see that you are a cleric by training, but based on the wear on your first two fingers of your right hand, that you are also an author. You love to write."

At this everyone cheered again. They all knew he was right - I really had no secrets in this town.

"You also recently returned from a short trip to Virden, the residue of red clay on your boots gives that away quite clearly."

I nodded, "yes, you are right."

"I'd also wager that with the four gold, three silver, and ten copper in your pocket that you might want to buy the next round of ale?"

The Inn erupted in loud cheers and laughter.

I dug into my pocket and brought out a handful of currency. I counted them out for everyone to hear. "Four gold, three silver, and…" I admit I was enjoying this. "One, two, three, four, five, six copper pieces."

The crowd went quiet.

"Are you sure?" he asked.

"I know how to count," I said, a little annoyed.

At this he laughed and slapped me on the back. What was it with humans and back slapping?

"Of course you do! I meant are you sure you got all of the coins? Perhaps check your other pockets?"

I reached into my other pants pocket, and pulled out a small ball of lint.

"That won't buy any drinks!" Someone yelled, and they all laughed.

"Make a wish!" Someone else yelled, and got even more laughter.

I reached into my jacket pocket and found something. I brought it out. It was more copper. I counted them out loud. "One..."

"You mean seven," Chaloner said.

"Yes, yes. Seven, eight, nine, and ten copper pieces."

Cheers erupted again.

Chaloner held up a hand. Everyone quieted down.

"But…" I said.

"Yes?"

"There's also a gold piece. That makes five gold," I said.

All eyes were on us. I held up the gold piece and showed it to the crowd.

Chaloner raised his voice and called out to the barkeep, "How much for a round for everyone?"

"One gold piece" he shouted back.

Chaloner snatched the coin from my hand before I could react. He tossed it across the room to the barkeep who caught it expertly.

"Like I said, four gold, three silver and ten copper!" Chaloner announced.

The place went wild. Most were cheering, others laughing. All were clapping. Chaloner gave me another affectionate slap on the back and directed me back to the table with Sir Locke.

Chaloner gave another bow. First toward me, then toward the barkeep. Then to the other areas of The Inn.

"I hope to see you all at the show tomorrow. If you don't show up, I'll know why!" He said this with a wide smile and a small wag of his finger. He backed his way to the exit, bowed once more, and left.

"What did you think?" I asked Sir Locke. I wondered if my friend would be jealous.

"Amazing really," Sir Locke said.

He seemed in deep thought. I felt bad for my friend. Up until five minutes ago, he was looked upon as the best, and only, detective in town.

"I don't know. He didn't do anything you couldn't do," I said. Not totally sure - I don't think Sir Locke could have deduced the amount and type of coins in my pocket and he knew me better than anyone.

"No, he did something I've never been able to do."

"What? Deduce the amount of currency in my pockets?" I asked.

"No. I've never gotten you to buy drinks for me, much less for the whole house," Sir Locke said with a hint of a smile.

"Well. I never…" I said, trying to feign insult.

"Exactly," Sir Locke said, not missing a beat.

The next day I wasn't surprised that my friend wanted to go to the carnival. I knew he wanted to see The Great Chaloner again.

The carnival had pitched their tents, four in all, in Jo Jevar's field. Since the harvest was a month ago, it made an ideal location. They paid Jevar ten silver a day and free passes for him and his family. I wondered why they went to Jevar first, why not one of the struggling farms? I thought a farmer with less would be eager to make a little extra money, even if it damaged their ground a little.

I asked Sir Locke about this and he said it was "because no one is tempted by greed more than the person who already has a lot. The more you have, the more you want."

The main tent dwarfed the other three, and was in the center of the field. You could see the flags atop the main pole from anywhere in town. Two of the other tents held "side attractions," and the last was where they kept the animals. They boasted the most exotic animals in the Empire, all in one place, under one tent.

Scattered throughout the grounds were hawkers with stands. Each hawker called to the crowds, enticing them to visit their stand where they could see amazing tricks, have their weight and or age guessed, play "find the pea", have their fortune told, or have a mystery solved. These went on throughout the day, and night, and filled in the time between the main shows in the tents.

I thought Sir Locke would go directly to the mystery solver, The Great Chaloner, but instead he went to the "Amazing Yorben, the Wizard of the Romani Clan."

A young boy was doing the hawking at this booth. The Amazing Yorben sat on a high stool in the booth, cross legged, unmoving. His wild blue hair matched his beard and mustache. His large shaggy brows were furrowed. He didn't look like a happy gnome, but a gnome he was!

Sir Locke went up to the booth. There were three eager customers ahead of him, so we waited in line. Each in turn placed their silver piece (the sign on the front of the booth read, "1 Silver per trick") in the box on the ledge of the booth and stepped around the side. They entered the booth and The Amazing Yorben closed the curtain. I couldn't see anything that went on in the booth, but when the second young customer was behind the curtain, brilliant lights shone through the sides, the top, and the bottom of the curtain.

The last customer ahead of us must have asked for an interesting trick. When she came out her hair was standing up all over, like she had been in an electrical storm.

Sir Locke approached the booth and said, "Can I ask you some questions?"

The Amazing Yorben just stared straight ahead. I nudged my friend and pointed to the sign on the front of the booth, the one listing the price. I found it hard to believe that my friend, a master of observation, had missed this.

"My mistake." He took out 1 gold piece and held it up. "I prefer information. Will this suffice?" He put it in the box.

The Amazing Yorben waved Sir Locke into the small booth and pulled the curtain closed.

When Sir Locke came out, he went over to the box, and put five silver pieces in.

"He deserved a tip? I thought 1 gold was more than enough."

"Oh, the gold was for information. The silver was for a trick or two."

"Really? So, you believe in magic now?"

"Of course, my dear Latswin. I believe you can heal without herbs or medicine, that potions can make you faster, and Druids can shapeshift into an animal. Why wouldn't I believe in magic? I'm actually planning on learning some myself. It could prove very useful in my detective work."

"What tricks?"

"I asked him to do Detect Magic on my competition, The Great Chaloner."

"And?"

"It turns out our detective is more magician than bard, although I will admit, he is a better showman than I."

"And you believe this Yorben fellow?" Since he was a gnome, I instinctively considered him more trustworthy than most, but, as I said, I had learned a valuable lesson in Virden. "Do you trust him? Don't these carney folk stick together?" I asked.

"Oh, he's new and I doubt he'll be sticking around," Locke said.

I looked at my friend with my customary inquisitive expression.

"Latswin, it really is elementary."

"Is it because of his grouchiness? He looks very gruff. Did you deduce that he was unhappy?" I tried.

"No. But you are right, he does look grumpy, doesn't he? Actually, I think that's his normal countenance."

I looked some more, trying to see what my friend saw. When I showed no signs of success, he explained.

"Look at the booth. See the hastily painted sign? You can see where it's been painted over numerous times. The booth is also the worst of the bunch. The hawker is a young child, while all the others have more seasoned workers. I surmised that his attraction is new to the carnival, probably on a trial basis."

"How did you know he wouldn't be here long?"

"He told me. He asked about work at the university and about our library. I'm guessing he'll be staying in town when the carnival leaves."

We started to walk away and I remembered, "what were the other tricks?"

"Ah, that was an advance," Sir Locke said.

"For what?" I asked.

"For a trick later today. You'll have to wait and see; I wouldn't want to ruin the show for you." And I couldn't get anything more out of him about it.

Our next stop was to see Chaloner.

It turned out that some acts in the big tents also had booths. This helped them build interest for their particular shows as well as earn them more money. It made for a very long day for the carneys, but the carnival only lasted for two or three days before they moved on.

We visited Chaloner's booth first. His booth was very fancy, with his image painted on the sides, and his name, "The Great Chaloner" on a sign above the booth.

There was a price list, prominently displayed.

Displays of reasoning - 2 copper

Minor Mysteries - 1 silver

Major Mysteries - 1 gold

Impossible Mysteries - 5 gold

I wondered what he would do for his act in the tent. Unlike Yorben the Magician, Chaloner did his act outside his booth, in front of everyone. He didn't mind having an audience - actually I think he thrived on it. Sir Locke suggested that I go buy myself some carnival food and drink. He was going to watch the Great Chaloner for a while.

So, I did.

Carnivals are more famous for their foods than their attractions. You can find the best foods from almost every ethnicity and region in the empire. And they are assuredly the unhealthiest foods you can find in all of Aethrofell.   Deep fried anything, candied corn, sweet wheat, and all kinds of chocolates.   Popcorns - caramel, pepper, cheese, and kettle.   Like a good party, the food was the most important factor in making it a success - and while carnivals tended to have a bad reputation for many things - food was not one of them.

When I returned with my hands full, Sir Locke came over to me.

"Is he done?" I asked between bites of my Candied Fleece.

"Yes.   He headed into the tent for his main show.   He puts on three a day and two at night, but I want to make sure we see this first one."

"Did you learn anything watching him?"

"A bit.   He didn't show too much.   He wants me to attend the main show."

"Are you sure?"

"Oh yes.   He isn't hiding it.   He actually called me out by name.   He claims that my detective skills are just showmanship." My friend seemed very calm for someone who was accused of being a fraud.

"And?"

"And, he challenged me to a competition.   It looks to be a big part of his show."

"Why give him what he wants?" I asked.

"My dear Latswin, the gauntlet has been thrown down, how can I let it lie there? I must pick it up!"

"So, should we go in to make sure we get a seat?" I asked.

"Oh, we'll have a seat.   My guess is Chaloner will have seats reserved for us."

So, we took our time. We walked around the grounds, me eating my haul, Sir Locke enjoying the different booths and attractions.

When we entered the main tent, the Great Chaloner himself met us at the entrance.

"Glad you could make it Mr. Holgrim, I have seats reserved for you and Mr. Gilshire up front."

He led us to the two front row seats.

There were three acts before the Great Chaloner. One included the largest wolf I had ever seen. They were all very entertaining and unlike the Gladiatorial games, these were family friendly.

When the Great Chaloner began his act, he asked for five volunteers from the crowd. These were all selected from the front three rows around the tent. After selecting four volunteers, the Great Chaloner announced, "And for our fifth and final volunteer please help me to welcome your very own, Sinben Locke Ariji Umji Merfiz Holgrim, better known as Sir Locke the gnome!"

Chaloner started clapping and applause rang up around the tent, growing until everyone in attendance was clapping and then standing. I got caught up in the excitement and joined in.

Sir Locke finally stood up and waved one hand to the crowd. He worked his way past all of the well-wishers until he got to the aisle and entered the ring with the other four volunteers.

Chaloner's act went pretty much like it did at The Inn the night before. The only difference was that this show had more flash and panache. Everything was done with a flourish and all deductions were announced and then repeated.

I recognized the first volunteer as the young gnome from The Inn, the one with the raucous friends. Sir Locke was right, he did propose to his girlfriend. Chaloner made a great show of it. Deducing that the young gnome had a question in his heart. That it involved a young female gnome, and that she was in the audience. He even deduced what she was wearing and then with a flourish he did his open palm gesture into the crowd. The spotlight followed his motion and stopped on a cute, shy young gnome. Cheers went up. She reluctantly came forward. Then the boy bent on one knee and reached into his left pocket.

Chaloner announced in a stage whisper - which means it sounded like he was whispering while he projected his voice so everyone in the tent could hear him - "The other pocket." Sure enough, the boy found the ring in his right pocket, and placing it on her finger, asked her to be his bride.

I thought it was romantic, and although she was obviously shy, she seemed to like it.

When she said "yes" (you could figure out what she said by the head nod and how the boy started jumping up and down and dancing around her) the applause from the audience was deafening. Somehow the two newly engaged youngsters found their way back to their seats.

The next volunteer, a portly female gnome, found out that her husband had been sneaking out at night to gamble with his friends. She didn't wait for the applause to stop. She balled her fists and started for the stands. There was a commotion as her husband pushed his way to the end of the row, leaped (he was only in the fourth row) to the ground and ran for his life. I was especially impressed by the woman's speed. I estimated she'd catch him well before they reached home.

The fourth volunteer had a much calmer revelation bestowed on him. He found out that his grandfather's heirloom, a jeweled dagger, was under a floorboard in his house, hidden there by his father before he died. The gnome was so grateful that he had to be pulled away from Chaloner. He wouldn't stop shaking his hand. When security (two burly humans) finally escorted him out of the ring, he ran off to find the missing keepsake.

Now there were only two "volunteers" left. One of our constables, Constable Droppkrag, and Sir Locke.

"You sir, are a constable, am I right?" Chaloner asked Constable Droppkrag. Since the constable was wearing his uniform, this got a good laugh from the crowd.

"Yes, yes I am" Constable Droppkrag said, loudly as if he were confirming a great deduction. This elicited more laughter.

"And you are here on official business, not pleasure," Chaloner announced.

"Yes, that's correct." Some more laughter, but not as much.

"You are looking into a crime. A report of a theft," Chaloner continued, looking around the audience instead of the constable.

"Right again!" The constable was impressed.

"Jevar, the owner of this parcel of land, our benefactor, the gnome who was so nice to allow us to pitch our tents here, he was robbed?"

The crowd became quiet. They hadn't expected anything serious like this.

"Yes. But how'd you…" the constable began, not as loud as before.

"How did I know? I'm the greatest detective in all of the empire!" Chaloner announced to the crowd. Some cheers erupted and then applause. When it died down, he continued.

"A hefty sum indeed - when you combine the proceeds from his recent harvest and now our meager donation for the use of his land."

"Yes, over 1,000 gold pieces." There arose an audible collective gasp by the crowd.

All this time Sir Locke stood patiently by. I expected him to solve the crime, to jump in and take over, but he just stood there quietly waiting.

"Well, I have solved your crime and can hand over the culprit to you this very night!" Chaloner announced. He made a sweeping gesture as he said this and then raised both hands up high. The crowd cheered him on. During the sustained applause, everyone looked around to see if anyone would try to make an escape before they were called out. No one did.

When the noise level fell enough for him to be heard, Chaloner continued.

"I've worked with Mr. Jo Jevar to solve this crime and he has assured me that he has not spent even one gold coin of what we paid him. And this is important because the coinage we used was newly minted coins of the realm. Coins that we have not used anywhere else. Coins that would demonstrate our thief's guilt." He built this up with considerable flair. I myself was mesmerized by his delivery.

But I noticed that Sir Locke was not. He was actually looking around the crowd. At first, I thought he was nervous, as if he were the one to be called out as the guilty party. But by his expression I realized he was looking for someone specific. His gaze settled on someone by a tunnel, and he nodded. I followed where he was looking and was surprised to see Stalard from Virden.

I looked back at Sir Locke, intending to get his attention, but he was once again scanning the crowd. By another entrance, he saw the large figure of G. Newnes blocking most of the aisle. He nodded at him and Newnes nodded back. I didn't think that was who he was looking for though. He continued scanning the crowd. He finally found who he was looking for, in the front row, half-way around the tent from me. Although he was a gnome in a sea of gnomes, he was easy to spot. His wild blue-black hair, flamboyant mustache and beard was enough. He was waving his arms around making shapes in the air. I could see his lips moving. Whatever he was saying or doing went unnoticed by most because of the show. But Sir Locke noticed and gave a small grin.

My friend returned his attention to Chaloner.

"Sir Locke…" the Great Chaloner began, "would you please…"

A spotlight actually appeared on Sir Locke. That was amazing in and of itself, but what was caught in the spotlight was more amazing. Sir Locke, as if part of the act, pulled back his cloak so that his vest and pants were readily visible to all. And flying out from his vestures was a small winged person. You might have thought it was a hummingbird, but the humanoid shape of a female was unmistakable, from any distance. And the wings fluttered, but only as fast as a butterfly's. The wings were translucent and shimmered with color. She was beautiful.

She was also caught in the act.

The crowd was shocked into silence. Chaloner was also speechless.

"Gladly!" Sir Locke shouted. His voice carried well enough, he had learned to project in Bard College, although he rarely had the chance to practice it. He rarely drew a crowd and never one of this size. Pretty much all of Little Thoracia was packed into the main tent.

"You are amazing, Chaloner! How did you know that this little thieving sprite would be trying to frame me at this very moment?" Sir Locke continued.

The hush remained.

The sprite disappeared. Just winked out of sight.

The spotlight shifted to Chaloner. Whoever was working the light knew how to keep the show going.

Before Chaloner could respond, the sprite appeared again, this time on Chaloner's shoulder.

An audible groan came from the crowd.

After a few beats, the sprite disappeared again. But the damage had been done.

"I'm sure if the good Constable Droppkrag were to inspect my pockets he'd find a few of those newly minted coins you mentioned," Sir Locke said to the audience. "But you'll find that those coins were not put there by my hands. They were put there by that sprite. That sprite which has helped you, the Great Chaloner...' Sir Locke pointed his open hand, palm up, toward Chaloner, "...to not only rob Jo Jevar but also a robbery in Virden, the last town this honorable carnival stopped in." He said "honorable" with sincerity and conviction, not sarcasm.

There was a rumbling sound rising in the crowd. It was an angry sound.

"This honorable carnival which has been besmirched by your thievery." Sir Locke continued. He had the stage now and wasn't going to relinquish it.

I looked around and saw that it wasn't only the crowd becoming agitated, but the carnies too. They were gathering at the exits.

"Unlike a real detective, the Great Chaloner used magic and a sprite, to make himself appear to have mastered the art of reasoning."

Realization was coming over the crowd, and the carnies. Even though most of us had never seen a sprite, we all knew they were like fairies, with a little more of a mischievous streak, and they could become invisible at will.

"You had your sprite listen in to conversations, to find out secrets. You also had her inspect the contents of your subject's pockets before you announced, miraculously, that you knew what was on their person." Sir Locke was gaining confidence. Instead of shouting he was now projecting his voice from his diaphragm. This was a great experience for a bard.

The crowd started to boo. A mostly eaten apple landed near Chaloner's feet. The spotlight whirled to highlight a sapling gnome, her hair in pigtails, wagging her finger at Chaloner. The crowd couldn't help it - still angry, they laughed at the little gnome's chastising of Chaloner.

Sir Locke waited for most of the laughter to subside, and for the spotlight to return to Chaloner.

"But that could have been, would have been, forgiven. We all know that most acts at a carnival are illusions. And we willingly agree to participate in the farce. We like being entertained."

I thought Sir Locke was going too far, and giving too much credit to our fellow gnomes. But the crowd continued cheering.

"But stealing from your host, Jevar, and then trying to frame a brother gnome is where we draw the line!" Sir

Locke finished with a flourish that I was especially proud of. It seemed Sir Locke had been watching Chaloner closer than I thought. He had learned a bit from the showman.

At this announcement, the crowd grew belligerent again. They imitated the little sapling, throwing food scraps at Chaloner. Not a lot, and only remnants like the mostly eaten apple; us gnomes don't waste food lightly. Constable Stalard came forward and with Constable Droppkrag took Chaloner into custody. As they led him out of the ring, the crowd cheered, the loudest applause so far.

I worried for a second that the carnies would try to defend Chaloner, perhaps try to free him, but they were clapping along with the crowd.

The Ringmaster (later I found out he was also the owner of the carnival) entered the ring. He walked over to Sir Locke, the only one left on "stage." The spotlight was on the Ringmaster.

"We promised you the Greatest Detective in the entire empire, and we have delivered! I present to you, your very own, Sir Locke the Gnome." He grabbed Sir Locke's wrist and lifted his hand up. The crowd cheered even louder.

Sir Locke bowed to the crowd, turning in all directions. Then waved and returned to his seat. I looked over to G. Newnes and he gave me a thumbs up. I nodded. Then I looked for the magician, Yorben, but he had left. Probably to go back to his booth.

"Next up is the Amazing Zed, is he human or is he a Bear?!"

The crowd settled back into their seats. The rest of the show went on without a hitch (except for when the froghemoth[10] swallowed its trainer, and then spit him back out after a lot of prodding). Personally, I lost my fascination with it. I guess I just wasn't innocent enough anymore to truly enjoy it.

Before we left, Sir Locke went back to the exotic animal tent. Although he said it wasn't anything more than a petting zoo (they actually wouldn't let you pet any of them - you might lose a finger or two), he spent a long time in the tent. When I joined him there, he was sketching pawprints.

"This may come in handy someday," was all he'd say at the time. I noticed he had a nice collection of sketches. Each page had a rendering of the animal, its height and approximate weight noted on the page, and what its paw or footprint looked like in the soft dirt. I shook my head. It seemed my friend definitely had more than one talent.

"This was a pretty remarkable case," I said, trying to get my friend to tell me how he had done it. I knew he liked to share his reasoning after a case, and this time he was uncharacteristically quiet on the subject.

"What made this case unique was that all of the information was directly in front of us. There were no hidden cabinets or secret messages. The challenge was seeing that which was not hidden," Sir Locke said, and that's all he would say. Knowing my friend as well as I do, I saw that he was still working something through his mind.

He was still lost in his thoughts that night at dinner. We ate with G. Newnes (he bought our meals), and I signed my first contract as an author. I considered myself more of a biographer than a writer of fiction, but Sir Locke insisted the stories be listed as mystery fiction. It was his only request, so how could I deny him?

---

[10] A froghemoth is an amphibious predator as big as an elephant

G. Newnes Le'Strand readily agreed. It seemed that he was happy to keep the secret that my good friend was really as good as I made him out to be in my stories. Maybe because he understood that it could hamper my friend's effectiveness, but I think it was because he liked Sir Locke. And, people like knowing things that no one else knows.

"Promise me you'll write about the Case of the False Detective!" G. Newnes said to me as I signed the contract.

I smiled at him. I liked the title. He turned out to be very good at book titles.

We ate a relatively quiet and uneventful dinner and headed to bed early. G. Newnes had a long journey ahead of him and my friend was still deep in his own thoughts.

The next morning, we had breakfast with Constable Stalard. "I'll be heading back to Virden with our prisoner after lunch," Stalard said.

"So, how'd you do it this time, Locke?" I asked. The food hadn't come yet, so I took the opportunity to get the details.

"Actually, I did very little Latswin. It was Constable Stalard who did all of the hard work," Sir Locke said.

"Now go on, Mister Holgrim. I can't get close to your reasoning powers." I think Stalard was actually blushing.

Sir Locke ignored this.

"Latswin, this was a very educational case for me. I learned that sometimes investigative work requires a more diligent, persistent, and scientific approach. It's not all observation and reasoning," Sir Locke said. I couldn't tell if this realization was a good, or bad thing, for my friend. Besides the occasional investigations he undertook to prove his deductions, he hadn't spent a lot of effort digging through the muck.

Sir Locke continued, "our friend here, Constable Stalard was faced with a perplexing problem. A theft had occurred in his town and all evidence pointed at a man he believed to be innocent."

Stalard nodded at this.

"Granted, he had no logical reason for this assumption, just a feeling in his feet," Sir Locke said. Humans said "gut" but gnomes consider their feet to be much more sensitive than their stomachs.

"This is true. I've known Mr. Jurrien for years and I could not believe the evidence, no matter how compelling it was. I just knew he couldn't be guilty," Stalard added, apologetically.

"So, he dug deeper. And finally, he found what he was looking for. Or more accurately, he didn't find it," Sir Locke explained.

"What were you looking for?" I asked Stalard.

"The rest of the money Mr. Jurrien was supposed to have stolen. We only found a few coins on him and a few more in his house, hidden in a box beneath his bed. But there were over 220 more gold coins stolen from three different homes," Stalard explained.

"Couldn't the victims have exaggerated their losses?" I asked.

"Very astute of you Latswin," Sir Locke offered.

"Yes, but we confirmed their stories, and I trust all three of them also. See that's the thing. We're a small town as you know, and everyone knows everyone else's business," Stalard said.

We nodded.

"I spent hours checking in every establishment in Virden," Stalard continued.

"For more claims of theft?" I asked.

"No. To see if Jurien had spent any of the ill-gotten riches in town," Stalard said.

"And none had. So, you decided to look at the one who solved the crime in the first place, the one who did so with remarkable speed and talent," Sir Locke said.

"And flair," I added.

"Yes. I don't know anyone who could have done what Chaloner did. He was able to even deduce where Jurrien had hidden the coins and how much he had on his person," Stalard said.

"You mean anyone other than Sir Locke," I offered.

At this Stalard looked down at his hands which were on the table.

"No. I mean even Sir Locke wasn't as good as this fellow Chaloner." He looked up at Sir Locke. "That gave me another feeling, that this Chaloner person couldn't be for real. I spent hours looking at every possible conclusion, and there weren't any. If Jurrien had stolen that much he would either have it on his person, hidden, or had spent it. And I could not figure a way that Chaloner could have deduced any of it, much less the exact count of coins," Stalard explained.

"Seems a bit stupid to me," I said.

The food arrived and we paused to allow the waitress to set the plates. When she had left, I noticed Stalard seemed a bit put off. Then I realized how what I had said must have sounded.

"Not you. No, I meant it was pretty stupid of Chaloner to show off so much. Why would he do that?" I asked.

Stalard at first relaxed, but then looked confused.

"I don't know. I mean, it was one of the main reasons I followed him here. He was just too good," Stalard said.

"Better than me," Sir Locke added.

"Yes," Stalard said.

"But he wasn't," Sir Locke said. "So, why risk it? Why did he do the same with trying to frame me here?" Sir Locke seemed to be contemplating this. I didn't want to interrupt his thought process, so I dug into my breakfast.

"We know Virden was his first run of his new act. He never claimed to be a detective until then," Sir Locke said.

"But how did you figure it out?" I tried to ask through the eggs and potatoes in my mouth.

"I did some of that old-fashioned detective work myself. Stalard visited me early yesterday morning, before we headed to the Carnival. He told me everything he knew," Sir Locke said. To this Stalard nodded. He took a sip of tea and took a few bites of food.

"I was especially impressed with his diligence," Sir Locke continued. "He is a very good investigator." At this Stalard smiled.

"While we were at the carnival, I found some old bills they used to post in town. Most of their advertisements were vague enough to be used more than once. It saved on parchment." Sir Locke said.

"You deduced that?" I asked.

"No. I asked. I did very little reasoning on this case, my friend. Good investigative skills are just as important as reasoning. If you don't gather enough information, your reasoning will be faulty. If you don't reason properly, you won't come to the correct conclusions." Sir Locke announced this with confidence. It was obvious he had been thinking about this a lot.

"One of the carnival kids told me, and showed me an old flier that proved it. Chaloner's act, before Virden, was a slight-of-hand, magic act," Sir Locke said.

"But why come after you?" I asked.

"Why indeed. It was folly. But I think he couldn't help himself," Sir Locke said.

"He thought us all fools," Stalard said, between bites. Finally, someone who enjoyed a good meal. Sir Locke's plate was still untouched as usual.

"Perhaps. But I think it was more his own need to perform. You were right Latswin, he is a much better bard than I," Sir Locke said.

I tried to protest, but the piece of bread in my mouth kept me from arguing.

"It's alright my friend. I'd much rather be a great detective than a great bard."

"So, he was showing off? But why did he frame Mr. Jurrien and why call you out? That's a lot of hubris for one man," Stalard said.

"That bothered me," Sir Locke said. "This Chaloner had been doing a little petty thievery through his act for months, but never anything this big. And never framing anyone," Sir Locke said.

I looked at my friend.

"I asked. I find that youth are very willing to share information, if listened to," Sir Locke said.

"How much did it cost you?" Stalard asked.

"Two silver," Sir Locke replied.

We all laughed.

"I think the explanation is clear enough. Virden was a practice run. I was the real target all along. Hence the claims to be the greatest detective in all of Aethrofell. A title which I am known to desire," Sir Locke said.

"Why would Chaloner want to hurt you?" Stalard asked.

"Oh, not Chaloner. He's just a pawn in this game. Someone put him up to it. I would wager Chaloner didn't follow the instructions accurately. The stolen gold was supposed to be found. All of it, to help prove Jurrien's guilt, and more so, to prove mine. But Chaloner was greedy. He figured he could pocket some extra wealth on top of what he was paid to frame me."

"Who wants to hurt your reputation?" I asked.

"I don't know," Sir Locke said. A phrase I had almost never heard him utter before, and rarely have I heard him say after.

"But he, or she, wants me to find out," Sir Locke said.

Stalard and I looked at each other, and then at Sir Locke.

"Remember when I said that everything was laid out in front of us? That nothing was hidden? I was wrong." Another phrase my friend rarely said, not because of pride, but because it was rarely true. "There was a much deeper and more diabolical hand at work, well hidden from view."

Sir Locke continued, "why send Chaloner to my own home town? Why claim to be the greatest detective in the Empire? And why use a bard? Why not just frame me quietly? it would have been much more effective. No, the person behind this wanted it to be loud, public, and flawed. It was a test. A test and a challenge." Sir Locke looked at us with a seriousness I only saw when he was on a case.

"I thought you solved this case?" I asked.

"No, Latswin. This case has only just begun!"

The End

Book Six

The Aether Stone

The Adventures of Sir Locke the Gnome

The Aether Stone

By Latswin Gilshire, Cleric

It had been over a month since I entered my final semester at University and the same span of time since I had seen (or heard from) my best friend, Sir Locke the Gnome. Locke had been on my mind for the last week. I hoped he was alright and wondered if he had finally found the fabled College of the Detective. This mythical school could only be joined by invitation.

Sir Locke believed you could also join the school if you identified a member or discovered one of their meeting places. By doing so, you would prove your worth and be allowed to enter the College

I blame this preoccupation with my friends' whereabouts and well-being, for my poor observational performance, of which you will soon witness.

As I was leaving my private room (being a senior had a few perks) a gnome in some sort of uniform came up to me. The pants were long and tight like a squire's. The shirt was a no-nonsense affair, long sleeved and white. The jacket, deep blue, double breasted, with shined brass buttons all over the place. On top of his head he wore a square looking contraption, the same blue as his jacket. He had a bulging wide sac hanging by a leather strap, on his left side.

Much too fancy for a government official.

"Gilshire?" he said.

"That's me. Who are you?" I asked.

"T. P. Ratchet, nice to meet you." He handed me a correspondence. The writing on the outside of the tri-folded paper looked like a cipher. It said 'Latswin Gilshire, Cleric. Gnome University, Little Thoracia, 3rd floor, 2RFS.' It was sealed with a dollop of red wax. I didn't recognize the signet used to set the seal, but the style (a magnifying glass and a sword in a circle) screamed of Sir Locke.

"How did you know where to deliver this?" I asked the gnome. He tipped his cap, and explained.

"Oh, I have devised a system. It involves names, locations, and something I'm calling "addresses." The key to the system is the Ratchet Directory where I track all current, and sometimes future, residences of everyone in Little Thoracia."

"What's 2RFS?" I asked. The rest of the information was clear.

"Second Room From Stairs," he answered a little sheepishly. "It would be great to have numbers on each door, but I haven't convinced anyone of doing that yet."

I nodded as if I agreed. I hoped he'd make a hasty exit.

Thankfully, he did.

The bag slung over his shoulder was full with other correspondence (he was calling them "letters").

"Sorry to run, I have more deliveries to make. Have a nice day!"

I went back into my room, deciding I needed some privacy before breaking the seal. I hadn't seen my friend in so long that I was sure I'd easily become emotional.

I shouldn't have worried, as the message was classic Sir Locke, which meant that it was direct, specific, and devoid of anything that could actually elicit emotion.

The "letter" said: *Latswin, I will be in need of your assistance in the very near future. In between your classes, please find time to carry out the following list of small, but critical, tasks.*

This was followed by a very concise list of tasks.

Of course, I had to figure out how to get the list of tasks done while keeping up with my coursework. My friend's concept of the time and effort required to do tasks was very inaccurate. It was undoubtedly exact if he were doing the tasks, but he projected his own habits onto others. It would take me a lot more than the free time I had between classes.

I decided the only way to get the tasks done in a timely manner would require a couple of days leave. I headed out to make this request from my lead professor.

Halfway across campus I was accosted by a filthy looking gnome. I would normally have avoided him, but I was a bit distracted.

"Can you spare a coin or two?" He was a small creature, bent over from age and what looked to be a bad back.

"A proper breakfast seems to be a more accurate assessment of your needs," I said, doing my best Sir Locke impersonation.

I missed my friend.

"Quite generous of you, governor." His accent was stinted. I guessed he may have been from Grimstone, the capitol. "Perhaps you could spare a hot bath to accompany the meal?"

I laughed heartily. I did not expect such brazenness, but from the look of him, I couldn't argue that he was in dire need of a good cleaning, a change of clothes, and a good meal.

Even though I was in a rush, I seriously considered helping him, if for no other reason than he had had the gumption to ask. But, I needed to talk to my professor if I was going to help my friend.

"I'm sorry but I'm in a rush…"

"Everyone seems to be. How long would it take to dig out a coin or two from your pocket?"

His persistence was wearing me down.

"But…" I tried.

"At least you took the time to talk to me. Thanks for that, mate." He turned to trudge off.

"Wait," I said and he stopped. He turned back to me. "Come with me," I said.

I led him back to my private room (with my private bath).

"You are too kind, governor. Thank you, thank you, thank you." He said, shaking my hand vigorously.

"It is my pleasure. I'll be back in a little while and we can get some breakfast." I led him into the bath. I handed him two towels (it was definitely going to require a lot of soap and water). I closed the door, giving him some privacy and headed off to see my professor.

Since I was in my last year and one of the top students, there was no problem in gaining permission for the short sabbatical.

When I got back to my room, the man was gone. I noted that the towels were dry. I checked my valuables, all the while chastising myself for being so gullible. But I couldn't find anything out of place or missing.

Perhaps something had come up.

I decided not to ponder it further. Unlike my friend, I could ignore a mystery. I had things to do.

The next day, I received a message from Sir Locke's mum, asking me to look in on him.

I was surprised that he had returned without letting me know.

In his letter to me, he hinted that he would be back soon, but according to his mother, and her network of friends, he had been back in town for nearly a week. Well before I received his communique.

While his apartment above the Baker's shop afforded him independence and the solitude he craved, he rarely missed an opportunity to visit with his mum.

Strange behavior indeed.

Latswin, be a dear, and check up on him. I don't want to come across as a mother hen. You know Sinben, he gets so focused on his hobbies that he can forget to eat.

She was the only one that called Locke by his given first name, Sinben.

If I hadn't been in the midst of classes (the one on herbal medicines was extremely difficult for me), I believe I would have noticed, without the prodding of his mother. I usually saw Sir Locke every couple of days, if for no other reason than to share a meal. Not much sharing actually as he ate so little - she was right about his appetite for food. He said he preferred to feed his mind.

I hadn't finished all of the tasks he had given me, but I had gathered some of the information and specific items he had listed.

I knocked on his door, but there was no response. I thought he might be in the loo, so I waited a bit. When I knocked again, I thought I heard a soft groan. Seeing as the door was unlocked, I let myself in.

The room was a mess, even for Locke's standards. He definitely supported the concept that a cluttered room was the sign of a cluttered mind, and a cluttered mind was a sign of genius. There were stacks of books (they must have cost him most of his earnings) around the room and drawings scattered across the floor. Vials and flasks filled one of the two tables. The other table had two open books, more drawings, and one lit candle in a holder.

A couch, a stool, and a comfortable looking chair rounded out the rest of the furniture.

I thought I heard another groan from behind the couch.

It turned out to be a snore.

Sir Locke was laying on a blanket, on the floor, fast asleep.

Being of medical training, I checked to see if he was asleep from natural means or if he was under a spell. The two things my good friend didn't do much of was eat and sleep. Finding him taking a midday nap was about as unexpected as him eating a whole shepherd's pie.

I was not surprised then to find a green liquid dripping from his slightly parted lips. I dabbed the liquid with my finger and examined it; first smelling it and then tasting just the smallest amount.

When I awoke, I found that I had fallen onto the floor, luckily, not on my friend who was still snoring beside me.

Lucky for him.

And lucky for me that I had only fallen a short distance as I had been kneeling beside him at the time.

From the light coming through the window, I deduced that I had been out for either an hour or 25 hours. I hoped it was the former.

I took out my pad and charcoal to make notes about the liquid, and noticed, under Locke's hand, a scrap of paper. I also noticed (too late) that there was a piece of charcoal by his hand, and his fingers had the dark residue from writing. I lifted his hand, extricated the paper and read his note.

I wasn't worried that it was some last rite declaration, my friend wasn't the type to hurt himself. No, I found what I was now expecting. Notes on the liquid he had consumed. It looked like a recipe.

60 parts Water
20 parts Nightweed[11]
10 parts Sallow powder
7 parts Ground Fey Spice
3 parts Mint

How he prepared it wasn't listed, only the ingredients. The smell, color, and taste all fit the ingredients, so I assumed he had drunk some of the potion he had made.

The *"why"* would have to wait.

There was no antidote listed. Nor notes on the potency or expected duration of the potion's effects.

I could do nothing but wait.

Well, that was not totally true. I decided to busy myself while I waited.

The first thing I did was shout out the window at the first sapling I saw on the street.

"What day is it?"

"Tuesday" he shouted back and went on his way without hesitation. I didn't want to ask an adult - they would have undoubtedly thought I was daft. Children assume little, and care even less.

---

[11] Nightweed, a plant found only in the Northern edge of the Bloodleaf Woods

I was relieved to find I had been out for only an hour.

I then took to tidying up the room. I like things to be neat and orderly. Put away. I also opened all of the windows to air out the place, hoping the fresh air would bring Locke around sooner. I didn't bother trying to get him onto the couch - he was taller than me (very tall for a gnome at 4 feet) and he had obviously planned out his experiment so that he spent his time on the blanket.

Based on the encroaching darkness and my grumbling stomach, I ascertained that my friend woke up around dinner time.

I heard his snoring stop with a cough, and then he rose to a sitting position on the floor.

"Latswin, my good man. I'm glad to see you," he said as if he had invited me over and he had just ushered me in. He shook his head slowly, and then faster, and then fast enough to make me worry.

"Locke?" I said, rushing over to him.

"I'm fine my friend. Just finishing my experiment," he said as he jotted down another note on the paper that had the recipe.

"Where have you been for the last week? Your mum's worried about you."

"Ah, yes. I will have to make amends with her. I likely owe you an apology also. I have been buried in my experiments and have forgotten the most important things."

"When did you start dabbling in alchemy?" I asked.

"Ever since our visit to Grimstone, and the poor demise of Tyann Rit. Like magic, I think alchemy can be very useful for a detective."

"So, have you given up completely on being a bard?" I asked.

"No, my dear Latswin. A bard I am and a bard I shall always be. But, it is the type of bard I am seeking to modify."

"So, you still think there's a 'College of the Detective' out there? A hidden school?" I prodded.

"It may not be a school; it could be a society or an association. The only thing I'm feeling confident of is that it is secret."

He looked around the room, seeming to see it for the first time.

"I see you've been tidying up," Sir Locke said.

"Yes, I, well. What was the experiment?"

"I'm sure you can deduce that, Latswin. You've already examined the ingredients and you've sampled the potion."

I wanted to feign indignation, but I wasn't surprised in the least that my friend knew all that and more.

"And thankfully you did not extinguish my candle." He looked at the candle closely. I noticed for the first time that it had markings on the side, like a ruler.

"hmmm, 12 hours. So how long were *you* out?" He asked me.

"I'm not sure, but I believe it was less than an hour." I didn't tell my friend that I had asked a passerby what day it was, not realizing that it couldn't have been a full day. I hadn't even thought to look at the candle.

"Was the effect immediate?" he asked.

"Yes, scarily so."

"And how much did you imbibe?" he asked.

"Just a taste on my tongue."

"Excellent!" He jotted down some more notes on his parchment. When done, he tossed it on the table. I doubted it would ever get filed away. It seemed that once my friend wrote something down, he no longer needed the document. It was forever locked in his brain.

"Dinner?" he asked.

"Sounds great," I said.

Sir Locke smiled at that.

"I thought so," he said. And I realized the rumbling noises my stomach had been making were reasonably loud.

We took the meal, a serving of mutton, cornbread, gravy, and kale, in his apartment.

"You've been gone for more than a month, and then you didn't visit your mother upon your return. I am not ashamed to say, I'm worried about you." I didn't think that I had ever spoken as earnestly with my friend in all the years that I'd known him.

He put down his cup of tea (a new libation that he had taken to drinking at every meal) and looked directly at me. I felt compelled to put down the gravy-soaked cornbread that was just touching my mouth.

"I am sorry, my friend," he said. Then he sipped his tea and looked away.

I sat still, staring at him. When my stomach growled at the interrupted rhythm of my meal, I broke the silence.

"That's all? You've been gone a month, you return and don't visit your mother, you don't explain your whereabouts…" I stopped. He had turned back to face me, his eyes and mouth smiling.

"Hmmph! Not humorous in the least," I chastised him. But I couldn't stay angry, I had to smile.

"I *am* truly sorry Latswin, but let me make it up to you," he said as he lifted his plate and using his fork, scraped his mostly untouched meal onto my plate. He stood up and clasped his hands together behind his back.

He began to walk around the room in the same posture as I had seen his father do many times before. I made a mental note to look into such behavior - was it nature or nurture?

"I will tell you all that has occurred. I will endeavor to relay the tale in a much shorter span of time than it took to unfold." His usual grin accompanied this small joke.

In response, I lifted the gifted leg of mutton, sat back, and nodded.

"As you know, I left Little Thoracia with Constable Stalard and our prisoner, Chaloner McCloundy, '*The Great Chaloner*.' I had reason to believe the Constable's journey back to Virden might be a little more eventful than he thought. I had numerous suspicions that Chaloner had been working for someone other than himself, and that his employer would want him silenced." Sir Locke paced the room.

"When we reached Virden without incident, I wondered if I was mistaken. I had spent the whole journey interrogating Chaloner, all the time keeping my eyes and ears attuned to our environment. I more than half expected an ambush or a rescue attempt," he continued.

I knew better than to interrupt him. I figured it was better to let him work through the story without interjecting any questions, and my stomach readily agreed.

"I learned a great many things from Chaloner, to which I easily concluded that I was correct, he indeed was a pawn in a bigger game. And that some unnamed benefactor had provided him with the where-with-all to frame me, mostly with the aid of Willow."

Although my stomach protested, I had to speak up.

"Willow?"

"Yes, my friend. Willowshimmer is the full name of the Sprite. Unlike Chaloner, she was able to escape capture," he added.

I nodded, remembering how Chaloner conned most of Little Thoracia into believing he was a better detective than Sir Locke. But it had been all misdirection and magic. And the key component to his con was the use of a fairy. The little creature could become invisible at will. With her help, Chaloner almost succeeded in destroying Sir Locke's reputation.

"So how were you mistaken?" I asked.

"It seems Chaloner was in no danger, and neither was Constable Stalard, nor for that matter, was I. However, I was still glad that I had accompanied them as it afforded me the opportunity to learn as much as I could about our antagonist."

"Chaloner?"

"No…"

"Willow, the Sprite?"

"No…" Sir Locke's grin returned.

I took another bite of mutton while I tried to figure out who he was referring to.

"The unnamed employer. The person who provided a Sprite in servitude with the express purpose of attracting my attention."

"Don't you mean with the purpose of framing you?" I asked. It was possible to speak with food in your mouth, but it took practice. I perfected this skill thanks to my friend's habit of providing expositions during meal times.

"No. I was doubtful at the time of the incident, but after speaking with Chaloner, I became certain. While Chaloner believed he would succeed, his benefactor would not have been as foolish. It was a simple test of my skills. Either it was designed to see if I was as good as your stories portray or it was a means of getting my attention." He walked over to the window. He peered down at the street below.

"Or perhaps both?" I suggested.

"Very insightful Latswin!" He seemed to think it over. "If it were only a test, then there likely would have been a subsequent communication. The mind behind this was not trivial. He went through considerable trouble, and expense, so a test for the sake of a test seems unlikely."

Locke walked over to the desk and absently picked up his cup of tea.

"And he would have expected me to pass, for Chaloner to be arrested, and for me to interrogate him. No, this was not simply a test." He carried his tea back over to the window. "And it wasn't just an attempt to get my attention."

"So, it *was* both!" I declared. I was proud of my deduction.

"In a way, yes." He stood quietly looking out the window for a moment, which his bard instructor would have called a 'dramatic pause.'

"This was an invitation."

I finished the mutton and turned my attention to the rest of the cornbread and gravy, wondering. What exactly was this 'invitation' for?

After we cleared the table my friend continued.

"Chaloner would provide no more information. I had to make a decision - either return to Little Thoracia and my research or follow the only lead I had, the only real connection to the mystery employer."

"But the Sprite was gone," I offered.

His smile affirmed that I had made a valid deduction.

"Yes, very good, Latswin. Willow was the key."

"But how could you find her?"

"As you know, I've learned a few tricks," he said. I looked at him a little dubiously.

"Yes, you are correct. I have not learned enough to track a Sprite. But our new friend Yorben taught me a spell for tracking an item."

Yorben, the magician from the Circus, had ensconced himself in the University Library. By all accounts, he ate as much and as often as Sir Locke. For the last month, no one had seen him outside of the edifice.

"Do you remember when she kept one of those bright, new coins they tried to frame me with?"

I nodded.

"There is a spell for tracing a specific item, especially if you put a magical marker on it. I had done so for all of the coins, which included the one she kept. Despite her orders. She couldn't help her nature - and she loves bright shiny things."

"After putting Chaloner in a cell in Virden, I waited for her to catch up. She did, and then continued on to Grimstone. I presumed she reported that Chaloner was in prison and she was to head off to her next assignment."

We had returned to the main room. I had taken up my customary seat and my friend stood leaning against the large desk.

"I was able to intercept her quite easily really." My friend took another coin from his pocket and flipped it through the air. It disappeared before my eyes.

"Wha? Now you do magic tricks?"

"Not really." He tossed some powder into the air and it sparkled a radiant blue. Some didn't fall to the floor. Instead, it outlined a small sprite hovering between us. Its wings fluttered so quickly they were barely perceptible, like a hummingbird's.

"Willow and I have become fast friends."

The sprite sneezed and wagged a finger at Sir Locke. She flew out the window, obviously unhappy that she was now glowing a visible bright blue.

When she had left, Locke closed the window.

"It was actually too easy." He said softly. "While I was able to track her, trapping her should have been a much tougher task. I believed then, as I do now, that everything she's done has been at the behest of her mystery employer."

"So, her next assignment was…"

"Me" Sir Locke finished my thought.

I took a desert muffin from my pocket. This was becoming a very interesting accounting.

"As you know, I've become somewhat of a linguist, but Faery is a language I haven't had any experience with."

"So how did you interrogate her?" I asked. "It must have been extremely difficult."

"Actually, it was quite easy. Barely an inconvenience."

"The interrogation?" I asked.

"That's the thing. I didn't have to interrogate her at all. She willingly offered information in exchange for more coins."

"Lucky break for you," I offered.

"You know luck is only the residue of design. And in this case that is more true than normal."

He pulled a very ornate carved pipe from a pocket and put it between his lips. He took two quick breaths and then breathed out slowly through the pipe. I was amazed to see smoky images rise up from the bowl.

I could see the city of Grimstone. The tall buildings were unmistakable.

"What is that?"

"A pipe I picked up on my way to Grimstone. It allows the bearer to make minor illusions."

I wondered at this. My friend never toyed with luxury or unproductive items. If it didn't have a useful purpose, he ignored it.

He looked at my face, and as was his custom, he read it perfectly.

"Oh, it's very useful. Especially when describing things. And it also has a way of distracting people."

I looked down and saw that he had removed my wallet from my jacket pocket and held it in his hand.

He tossed it to me.

"But what does that have to do with the Sprite? Or the Sprite's employer? Or…"

"Forgive me the theatrics, my old friend. I did want to show it off. But, it was also a good way to highlight the fact that this case was full of illusions. From the start to finish."

"So, it's over?"

"No, not nearly." Locke said.

"So, what happened next?" I asked, wanting desperately to write it all down, but refraining from doing so, for the moment.

"We struck a bargain, Willow and I."

"And you trust her?"

"I trust her to carry out her employer's wishes."

I admit, that confused me.

"She led me to Grimstone and to a young, pretty gnome named René Dupreau."

I was getting pretty good at reading body language also, and I could see that my friend found this René to be more than pretty.

"I tried following this gnome, but she was very, very good."

"Good at what?" I asked.

"Oh. She's a thief. Of the highest caliber."

I thought perhaps that's why he seemed so excited when he mentioned her name. My friend had long desired to learn the rogue's trade. He felt it would help in his investigative adventures. Meeting one of such high skill must have intrigued him greatly.

"She gave me the slip easily. Luckily, before she did, I convinced Willow to plant a coin on her. So, I was able to find her using the locate spell. Quite handy for detective work."

"It would seem," I said.

"When I caught up to her, she was somewhere in the Emperor's palace. With considerable effort, guile, and a little bit of spell casting, I was able to follow her into the depths of the palace without being seen. Just as I was closing in on her, alarms sounded throughout the grounds."

I leaned forward, wishing more than ever that I had my journal.

"I was sure that she had been found out. I was confident that my own entry had gone unnoticed. But now that the alarm was sounded the palace filled with Dragonborn guards running all over. I barely escaped notice and possible capture."

"Lucky!" I exclaimed.

He shook his head disappointedly.

I nodded, but only to placate my friend's vehement distaste for the vagaries of luck, the concept of destiny, and the intervention of the gods.

"René also escaped and I was able to track her due to the coin and the spell. She was traveling much faster than I thought she could, so all I could do was follow."

"Did she succeed?" I asked.

"Good question. I heard rumors in Grimstone and on the roads out of the city that an Aether Stone[12], one of five within the castle walls, had been stolen. A country-wide search was quickly initiated."

"So, she succeeded," I said.

"Based on her quick exit out of the city, her obvious abilities, and the respect I've gained for my adversary - yes, I'd say she succeeded."

My friend paced the room again. This time he puffed out the image of a very attractive female gnome holding a round glowing orb.

"So, you saw her with the stone?" I asked.

He seemed surprised and bewildered. Then he looked up at the smoke illusion and used his hand to disperse the image quickly.

"No, no. I saw her. And I heard many descriptions of the Aether Stones. Turns out they are extremely powerful magical artifacts. However, I don't think a rogue, even of her abilities, has much use for one."

"So, she took it to sell it?"

"No, I'm sure it was her mission," he said.

"So, it was, what did you call him? Your adversary? Is he a wizard?" I asked.

"Very good Latswin. But you are jumping to conclusions."

---

[12] It is believed there were 15 magical stones created by the original races in Aethrofell to protect the country from invasion

"But he must be a magic user of some type. A wizard, warlock, or mage, right?"

"Well, there are also clerics and bards who are heavy magic users."

"Could this René be the mastermind?" I asked.

"No. Remember, we're looking for a heavy magic user."

"Perhaps the magic user works for her," I offered.

He smiled at me.

"No. He is a he, at least as long as Willow didn't lie about that. She referred to him as "he" more than once. She wouldn't give me a name, but she didn't hide his gender."

This time his pipe produced an image of my university.

"No!" I said, a bit too strongly.

"Unfortunately, yes."

Sir Locke filled me in on some of the details, but for the most part it was a tedious return journey to Little Thoracia. He couldn't tell who at the University René Dupreau had visited or if she had, as of yet, turned over the Aether Stone. He did know that she was still in town. She had a room at The Inn.

Locke had been working for two days (his mum's description of a week was an exaggeration only a mother could get away with) trying to prepare for what promised to be his greatest challenge yet.

A high-level magic user, likely a professor or teaching assistant at the University, was a brilliant enough mind to manipulate my friend for a month.

And he had orchestrated the theft of one of the most powerful magical artifacts in the kingdom, from under the control and security of the nation's Capital. He had dared to steal from the Dragon Emperor himself!

This would be no ordinary test of my friend's considerable talents, skills, and abilities.

And I knew, before this was all over, he would be in need of more than just my help.

"Did you finish your list?"

I had totally forgotten about the list of tasks he had sent me.

"Not all of them. I have the information on the faculty and…" I stopped. "That's why you wanted the list of faculty!"

He only smiled at me.

"I also got some of the ingredients you wanted." I pulled them out of my pockets, putting the odd assortment of herbs, minerals, and other items on the table.

He brushed his fingers over the items. Before he could ask I snatched up the other desert muffin from his grasp.

"Sorry, that's mine," I said.

"Very good!" Locke said, ignoring my rescue of the muffin.

"It wasn't that difficult, just a shopping list really," I said.

"Oh, I meant that you deduced they are ingredients. It's one more potion I wanted to try and I was hoping you could get them for me," he said.

I handed him the list with all but two items checked off.

"Are they important?" I asked.

"We should be able to do without them."

"So, what's the plan?" I asked.

Sir Locke always had a plan.

"We need more information Latswin," my friend said as he put a small cork onto a vial of green liquid.

"Who is the employer? A most important question." He said. "What does he need the Aether Stone for? It was definitely not a simple theft for profit. He wanted a specific stone for a specific purpose - I wager my life on it," he continued.

I hoped it wouldn't come to that.

"Where does René Dupreau fit in?" He added.

I believed my friend hopcd she was just a hired rogue. I believed my friend was smitten at first sight. I don't think he would have believed it, but I had had my own share of romantic adventures and knew it was only a matter of time.

My friend continued his introspection, talking to himself.

"Why involve me? Why risk his plans by bringing me into it?" This one he mulled over the most.

"Maybe he doesn't know how good a detective you are?" I asked.

"Even if I were the worst detective in the world, it wouldn't be a reason to bring me into the picture," he said.

"But if you were the greatest detective in Aethrofell?" I asked.

"That actually might make sense, Latswin. I have found that there are only two real motivators for crime, selfishness or hate."

"What about gold? Aren't most crimes because the criminal wants what he doesn't have?" I asked.

"Copper, silver, gold, platinum; they're all the same. Wealth. Riches. All of these are manifestations of greed.

The desire to have more. And greed is born of selfishness."

"But that can be said of almost everyone," I offered.

"True. Motivations are not unique to criminals. The means of satisfying those wants are."

"Ok, how about fame? Glory?"

"Still greed. These are just different forms of wealth," he said.

"Ok, how about love? Many crimes are done out of love." I wondered what my friend thought about the concept, especially in light of the way his eyes lit up when he spoke about the Dupreau woman.

"No, not love. Although some who commit crimes like to claim it as a cause. No, my friend. I am certain that true love would never lead to violence, theft, vandalism, or any criminal act. These are actually due to hatred."

"Seems a bit harsh. How about the man, or woman, who kills their competition?"

"Oh, that's greed again. It's just disguised as jealousy. Wanting something that you don't have. I was thinking more about revenge or uncontrolled anger. They either hate their victim, they hate who they are or what they represent, or in most cases, they hate themselves."

My friend had lost me and he could tell.

"The point is, my dear Latswin, that this 'employer' either wants what I have - the fame brought on by your silly stories, or he has some gripe with me. But I cannot for the life of me think of anyone that fits the bill."

"Locke, there are a lot of people that hate you. You've thwarted many a villain's plans."

"Of course, Latswin. I meant no one that could pull this off. No one we've encountered is this clever, patient, or determined. No, this is someone new." Locke said.

Again, my friend was right.

"There's only one source of information we're sure of," Locke said without enthusiasm. I'd never seen him so reluctant.

I waited, watching. He would tell me sooner or later.

"The sprite?" I finally tried.

"You are correct, the sprite does know more than she's told us, but Feywild are a different species. I can't get anything out of her she doesn't want to share. On the other hand, though, my recent concoctions work quite well on gnomes." To point this out, he picked up a vial that he had corked earlier. It had a deep green liquid. Then he picked up two other vials, a purple and a blue. He juggled them expertly.

"No, I was thinking of Miss Dupreau," Locke said

"Yes, it seems you have been," I said with a smirk. As usual, my friend ignored the inference.

"I think I could discern if she lied to us, but I can't think of a way to force her to answer at all."

"Could you threaten her with arrest? You said she stole from the Emperor," I offered.

"No one knows it was her. And I'm sure she no longer has possession of the stone. No, we need to use guile."

I smiled at this. My friend had never been good at deception.

"This is not your forte," I said.

"I have learned a thing or two while away," he said.

I looked at him.

"I visited you earlier," he smiled.

I thought a bit and then laughed.

"You were the gnome with the letters!"

"No, no. I could never contrive such a ridiculous disguise, and I'm not clever enough to devise anything like his system."

"Oh, I don't know. You're pretty clever," I said. I was a little disappointed that I had guessed wrong.

Locke waved his arms around, drew back, circled once and said something in a language I didn't know. Then he hunched down. When he looked up at me, now shorter than I, he was a dirty, unkempt, beggar. The man who I had offered the use of my bath.

"How…?"

"Wha', governor? Didn't you recognize me the other day? I believe you still owe me a breakfast." He laughed at his own joke. With another, much smaller gesture, his appearance changed and he once again was my life-long friend.

"How?" I repeated.

"As I said, I've learned a thing or two."

And that's when I had an idea. For the first time in our relationship, I had a solution to something that had stumped my friend.

"I know how to get this Dupreau gnome to tell us who her employer is without your concoctions."

The next day we put my idea into action. As you probably guessed, Sir Locke modified it quite a bit, but he still gives me the credit.

We spent the previous night preparing for the ruse.

First thing in the morning, Locke used his 'Disguise Self' spell to make himself look like T. P. Ratchet. His clothes even mimicked Ratchet's down to the fancy buttons. The disguise included the ridiculous hat. That was strange enough, but what disturbed me the most was how his physical appearance also changed. He seemed to shrink from his 4-foot frame to a more normal three and a third feet, his facial features changed, and even his hair color.

I, of course, used magic for my clerical spells, but for some reason I had trouble getting used to my friend using spells.

He stuffed a carry-bag full of the papers, folded and sealed that we prepared the night before. On each was written the name of a different male faculty member.

"I'm off," Locke said, sounding like Ratchet. I knew his voice acting wasn't magical. It was part of his Bard training. Perhaps a Bard *was* the best career for a detective.

After a brisk walk over to The Inn, Locke approached the front desk.

"Delivery for René Dupreau," Locke said.

The older gnome looked up from his breakfast. It was fruit and a cup of milk. Locke also noticed the gnome's dark pallor and blue tipped fingers. He looked miserable and unlikely to be helpful.

"My mum uses Orcberry[13] root to treat ulcers," Locke offered.

"Does it work?"

"Without fail. Boil the root and drink the residue like tea."

"Thanks! I'll try anything. This thing is horrible," the gnome said. He looked through his ledger and gave Locke the room.

"Hope I haven't missed her," Locke said.

"I would think not. She was out late last night and just got in a few hours ago."

---

[13] Orcberry is a wild fruit with a very bad aftertaste

"Thanks," Locke said and bounded up the stairs to the second room on the right past the loo.

At the top of the stairs, he reached into his bag and prepped the papers (Ratchet called them 'letters').

He knocked briskly on Dupreau's door.

He knocked two more times before Dupreau opened the door.

"What in the world…" she started. She was in a nightgown that flowed all the way to the floor. Her mane of red hair was a mess, and she was wiping sleep from her eyes.

"Delivery for René Dupreau," Locke announced. He pulled the letters from his bag and fumbled them expertly onto the floor. They covered her feet.

"Oh, I'm sorry…" Locke said as he bent over. Dupreau did the same, bending over and they bumped heads. They fell backwards onto their bums. They rubbed their foreheads simultaneously, and each said "ow" at the same time.

They looked at each other and laughed.

"Ow, ow, ow." René Dupreau said, now holding her head.

She laughed again, and then groaned.

"That actually made it worse," she whispered.

"I'm sorry." Sir Locke said again.

"Shhh. Not so loud," she said, rubbing her temples.

"My system is all messed up. I'll have to go back and figure out which goes where," he whispered.

He shifted to be on one knee and pulled his bag around to the front of him. He started putting the letters back in his bag.

"I'll bring your letter back in a while…once I figure it out," he said.

"Take your time. I'm going back to bed," she said, not getting up. She sat, leaning forward, with her head between her knees.

He stood up and backed out of the room.

"I'm very sorry," he whispered again.

She waved him off.

Locke left. He hurried back to his place over the Baker's. He had to hurry. He felt time pressing in on him. He didn't know exactly why, but he felt that time was of the essence.

He rushed into the room.

I was waiting for him.

He tossed the contents of his bag on the floor. We went through them quickly.

"So, we need to find…"

"Which one is missing." Locke finished my thought.

"Airity. Professor Mauri Airity." Locke announced.

I sat silent, shocked. And then it all made sense.

"It's him," I said. "He's been my mentor for the last two years."

"Hmm," was all Locke would say.

"You're right. He's a genius. And patient. He didn't ask me anything about you until I brought you up. It was a casual conversation. I told him about my hobby. I told him a lot about you."

We were silent again.

"It's not your fault." Locke said. "But I fear we don't have time to make you believe that."

I had my assignment, one that was not easy for me. I had been putting on extra pounds, I believed it was due to Sir Locke's inability to finish his meals. Running to get the constable and the mayor meant running to the other end of town, something I now believe my friend calculated in detail. There's little he doesn't think out so I would not be surprised if he tasked me with getting the authorities to keep me out of harm's way.

When I finally entered the halls of the University with the Mayor and Constable in tow, we were also accompanied by the President of the University who saw us coming from afar.

I went straight to my mentor's office and dramatically pushed both doors open with a flourish.

No one was in the office.

No Professor Airity. No Sir Locke.

"He's supposed to be teaching," the University President announced in a loud voice. We all took off down the hall, down a flight of stairs and down two more halls. As we approached the lecture hall, a bell rang three times. It was the large bell that tolled the start and end of classes.

As I reached for the double doors they burst open and we were engulfed by students rushing off toward their next class.

We fought like salmon swimming upstream.

Being the closest to the doors, I could see into the room. I saw one student sitting in the second row, engaging in debate with the Professor who stood behind a podium.

I could not hear what was being said, but I recognized the student to be my friend, Sir Locke.

"Professor Airity!" The University President announced when he made it into the room, a few steps behind me and the Constable. The Mayor cautiously peered in from the hall, keeping the door ajar.

Airity looked up from his conversation with Sir Locke. My mentor of the last two years and presumably the mastermind behind a lot of mischief, was a thin gnome easily twice as old as Locke and I. He wore the long formal robes of a Professor Emeritus. His hair was worn like a youth long, and pulled back into a ponytail. He was the epitome of the academic stereotype.

"President Billowheart, how can I help you?" Airity said without the slightest hint of fear or worry.

The University President stopped coming forward. He seemed lost, not sure how to proceed.

Constable Droppkrag didn't hesitate though, he went straight to the podium and the deep blue orb sitting on a woolen cloth.

"Is this the Emperor's stolen Aether Stone?" He stood pointing to the orb. The best I could tell, he was afraid to touch it. I didn't blame him that bit of caution.

"The Emperor's what? Did you say Aether Stone?" Airity said with his hand on his chest.

"Do you mean to say you haven't heard about the theft in Grimstone one week ago?" The constable was on a roll.

"Sorry Constable Droppkrag, news, as it were, doesn't travel that fast and I have my classes to focus on. Mr. Gilshire, I thought you were on sabbatical. Oh, is that The Mayor also?"

The president regained his footing and walked up to the podium. He took out his spectacles and examined the orb without touching it.

"Where did you get this?" The President asked.

"What did you think it was?" The constable asked.

For my part, I took my cue from Sir Locke and said nothing.

"Who gave this to you?" The constable asked.

"How long have you had this?" The President asked.

Sir Locke continued to sit, with his legs stretched out. He just watched the events unfolding, literally, in front of him.

"A merchant brought it to me yesterday. He said it was a family heirloom and he wanted its value assessed. And I am still analyzing it to determine exactly what it is. I'm sure it has powerful magic within it, but I don't want to jump to conclusions. I need more time to research it," Airity said.

I'm not the greatest at reading body language or discerning if someone is lying, but even I could see that the professor was laughing at us. He wasn't even trying to hide his deceit or contempt.

"What is the merchant's name?" Sir Locke finally spoke. I would have said he 'spoke up,' but he never raised his voice. Even so, his tone and tenor demanded attention. He stood as he asked and strode up to Airity.

"I don't see what his…" Airity began.

"Well, we will need to arrest him since he was in possession of the stolen Aether Stone. Perhaps he was the thief."

"No, no. He is a nice old gnome. A merchant I've known for years."

I thought about how my friend changed his appearance using Disguise Self. I would never consider eyewitness accounts as useful again.

"That's a lie. As pretty much everything is that you've said so far. Perhaps the need to research it further is true, but everything else is categorically and completely false."

"Mr. Locke, why would you say such things?" Airity asked, with that same laughter in his eyes.

"That's *Sir* Locke, professor." I burst out. "Shame on you. Even I can tell you're lying." I couldn't help it.

This gnome had been my mentor for two years and he had used me.

It took some time for the University President to round up three capable professors to wrap and box up the Aether Stone. None of the authorities wanted to touch it. I wasn't sure if it was due to the power of it or because they didn't want the Emperor somehow to know they had touched it.

In the end, they wrapped it in two thick woven cloths, and then placed it in a heavy wood and metal chest.

The constable arrested Professor Airity. Since the professor was an experienced cleric he was bound and gagged. The consensus was that the Emperor's Council would determine the professor's guilt or innocence. He was obviously going to stick to his ridiculous story.

He stuck to the story even when Sir Locke produced two long red hairs from Airity's jacket, hairs that matched René Dupreau's. He never produced a name for the merchant, or even a description. The most important evidence of his guilt was the lack of something, rather than the existence of it. He had no notes about the stone. Sir Locke argued if he had been examining it for a day and trying to determine its worth, he would have made notes. But Airity could not produce any.

When they went to arrest Dupreau and question her, she had already left town. They couldn't find her anywhere.

Sir Locke offered to once again travel with the constable, all the way back to Grimstone, but that turned out not to be necessary. The constable planned to start the journey the next day. The journey would require a deputized set of guards (Sir Locke would be one of them), a wagon, ponies, and rations for the trip as it would be a long journey.

But the next morning, the town was abuzz with excitement as a cohort of the Emperor King's Dragonborn Guard went straight to the town's main building where The Mayor and Constable Droppkrag welcomed them.

After a very short discussion, there was a transfer of the Aether Stone and the professor.

The Mayor and Constable took full credit for the arrest and recovery of the stone. Not a mention of Sir Locke or myself. I didn't mind not being included, but I thought it very poor form that they didn't give any credit to my friend.

"I don't need any more recognition, Latswin," my friend said over lunch that next day. We were celebrating, privately (just the two of us), the recovery of the Aether Stone and the capture of Professor Airity. Locke was actually happy. And I thought his happiness was in part because René Dupreau got away.

"How about the reward? I heard the Dragon Guard gave it to the constable and The Mayor." I tried.

"Just think of all the good will that will earn us," Locke said.

"But you tracked the Stone here after finding that Dupreau woman," I argued. "And without you they would never have found it!"

"Never is a long time, my friend."

"But it's not right," I insisted.

"What did you say?" My friend's demeanor changed suddenly. Drastically. I wondered what I could have said to turn his mood so completely.

"I said that you deserved credit…"

"No, after that."

"I said it wasn't fair…"

"No, actually you said, '*it's not right.*'"

"Well, yes, but…"

"How could I be so stupid?" he asked. I assumed it was rhetorical because my friend was anything but stupid.

"You're the smartest gnome I know," I said, trying to cheer him up.

"And that's the problem. I started believing all the silliness you've been writing about me. Oh, how could I have been so stupid?"

"I don't understand."

"No, my friend, you don't. But it's because unlike me, you don't have a hubris bone."

"What's that?" I was sure I hadn't slept through the section on gnome anatomy.

"It's the small bone that gets caught in your throat, the bone you choke on. I thought I was the smartest gnome in Little Thoracia."

"Hmmph. You *are* the smartest gnome in Little Thoracia. Probably the smartest in all of Aethrofell." I said.

He patted my shoulder.

"Yes. I may be the smartest gnome, but the fact that I know it blinded me to the truth. If I was less confident, if I had a smidgen of your humility, my good friend, I wouldn't have made such a colossal mess of it all."

"What are you talking about?"

"You said it - they may never have found the stone without our help."

"That's what I've been telling you," I said.

"And I should have listened."

I had no words.

"I'll explain it on the way," he said.

"Where are we going? Lunch is just being served." Indeed, I could see the waitress coming out of the kitchen with our meals.

"We need to get to Grimstone as soon as possible. Before the Aether Stone if at all possible."

"How are we going to do that? The Dragonborn Cohort is riding on horses and they have at least four hours head start. We couldn't catch them with a flying carpet."

"We need someone to teleport us there. We need someone who can *really* do magic. Time to go back to your university."

"Clerics can't teleport."

"No, but wizards can." He said as he grabbed my arm and pulled me to my feet. "We must hurry."

On the way to the university my friend explained.

"What did you notice when Airity was arrested?" he quizzed me as we ran.

"He's a terrible liar. With my little skill, I could tell."

"Exactly! What else?"

"He's equally bad at stealth. The stone thing, the orb, was right there."

"And?"

"I guess he's not half as smart as we were giving him credit for."

"Excellent work Latswin. Now tell me, you had him as a professor and he was your mentor for nearly two years."

"Yes, yes." I said. I was starting to have trouble speaking. Two days in a row of running was taking a toll on me. But I pushed through and continued for him, "but…he isn't an idiot. He's very, very, smart. And if what you said was correct about the complexity of his plans against you…"

"Exercise is good for critical thinking. The extra oxygen and increased heart rate are improving your mental capacity," he said.

"So, it was a ruse. He wanted to get arrested."

"Yes, Latswin. Excellent!"

And then a truly original thought came to me.

"Who contacted the Dragonborn Cohort? How did they get here so fast?"

"That was me I'm afraid."

"Brilliant Locke!"

"Not really. I sent Willow to alert them. I wasn't sure if she was totally loyal to Airity. I sent her as a test," he said.

"And she passed. She got the guards," I said.

"That was my first error. I thought she had passed the test," he said.

"Well didn't she?"

"Yes. But she didn't do it for me, she did it for Airity. I thought I was proving that she wasn't his puppet, but in reality, it proved exactly the opposite."

At the moment, I didn't think my brain was working better at all.

"He not only wanted to be caught, but he wanted to get to Grimstone quickly," Locke said.

"So, if he wanted to get to Grimstone, why not confess?"

"Because they might execute him on the spot. Or leave him to our honorable constable, leave him in our modest jail. No, by not admitting anything, he is guaranteed to be questioned by the emperor's inquisitors."

"So, he wanted to get to Grimstone?"

"More importantly, he wanted the Aether Stone to be returned, and returned quickly."

"Is that all?" I asked, amazed.

"No, Renee Dupreau also gave me a clue that I totally missed," he said.

"But she was the reason we knew it was…"

"Exactly! And as soon as she had done her job of pointing us to Airity, she disappeared. Why was she hanging around? Her job was done, the Stone was delivered. Why was she available?" he asked.

"To make sure you found Airity?" I offered.

We made it to the gates of the university and turned right. We headed directly to the library.

"Yorben?" I asked.

"Yes, my friend. Your deductive reasoning is coming along nicely."

"But I still don't understand why Airity wanted to return the treasure he worked so hard to procure."

"That's the real question my dear friend. 'Why' indeed."

We rushed into the library and headed directly to the main desk. The old gnome working the desk pointed to the section on arcane magic.

"He's been there for days. I don't think he ever leaves."

We raced through the aisles until we found Yorben in an alcove reading two books at once.

"Yorben, I once again need your assistance. This time, the fate of Aethrofell rests in your capable hands," Locke said.

I had always thought of him as a mediocre bard, but the more I observed the more I realized he was actually quite good. Just not in a classically entertaining way.

Although I thought his skills of persuasion were excellent, it seemed that Yorben, the wizard we met at the carnival (see the Case of the False Detective), was immune to a bard's wiles. It would take more than good intentions to convince Yorben to leave his research.

"Can't you just teleport us to Grimstone?" I asked.

"No." Yorben didn't speak much, and when he did I couldn't make out half of what he said due to his thick accent.

"He would have to travel with us," Locke explained.

"Okay. So, we go and then he can teleport himself back, right?"

"No," Yorben said.

"It can take hours to cast the spell and it would wear him out. He'd need to recover," Locke explained.

"So, he won't help us?" I asked.

"He will if we can offer him something valuable enough to make it worth him losing a day or two of his research. He's a very single-minded individual," Locke said.

I held back the urge to laugh. Looking at the two of them, total opposites and yet so much alike. Yorben was small, even for a gnome, with wild blue-black hair, beard, and mustache. His head was mostly hair with eyes, a prominent nose. You wouldn't know he had a mouth except that the occasional utterance revealed a mouth. But at that moment I'd swear they were long lost twins.

"How much gold can we get together?" I asked, mostly to keep from laughing.

"Not enough. He doesn't want coin. He wants knowledge."

"So, he won't help us?"

"Only if I agree to help him later with finding and gaining access to Gwendolyn's Tower."

"What's that?" I asked.

"I don't have the faintest idea," Locke said, frustrated.

"So, are you going to agree?" I asked.

"I don't believe I have a choice."

It was at this moment that I learned that my good friend, Sir Locke the gnome abhorred the unknown. I knew he had a driving desire to uncover any and every mystery that crossed his path, but I started to see the reason. He really couldn't deal with the unknown. Agreeing to assist in a quest that he knew nothing about was one of the hardest things he had ever done.

Of course, he agreed. His personal aversions to the unknown (no matter how dangerous they may be), couldn't excuse him from his responsibility to save the kingdom.

It didn't help that he was blaming himself for the entire situation.

It took Yorben a little less than an hour to prepare the spell. Since we knew it would take time, we went back to Locke's room and geared up. Locke took six of his vials with newly mixed concoctions, and just one dagger.

"Should we take a rapier? And a bow? or..." I started blabbering.

"No. We won't be doing any fighting," he said confidently.

For myself, I took extra parchment and graphite. I needed to start writing all of this down lest I end up having to embellish to fill in the parts I was bound to forget. Contrary to my friends teasing, I took pride in the accuracy of my accounts of his exploits.

I also grabbed some road rations, just in case.

When we returned to the library, Yorben ushered us to a small room on the lower floor of the building. The rumors were wrong (as almost all rumors are), Yorben did indeed sleep. The room contained a pile of rugs set up as a makeshift bed. There were a few books and scrolls at one end beside a mostly spent candle.

Yorben closed the door behind us.

"I will begin," Yorben said in his thick accent.

I understand magic and spells.

As a cleric I use them all the time. Especially for healing. Some are very powerful and require expensive materials.

But the spells Yorben used were beyond my comprehension. Like the teleportation spell he wove. We all sat in a tight circle while Yorben seemed to do, well, nothing. He seemed to be simply meditating. I expected him to sprinkle dust over an open flame (it would put the candle to use), jiggle some talismans, and make wild hand gestures. All while chanting rhythmically until he reached a loud crescendo, and "poof!" We would all disappear and reappear in Grimstone. Perhaps at the feet of the Emperor King himself.

But none of that happened.

We just sat quietly in the circle.

Thirty minutes later, Yorben opened his eyes.

"Sorry, needed quick nap," he said.

He proceeded to say five words softly. Too softly for me to make out what they were.

My eyes blurred. Or perhaps it would be more accurate to say our surroundings blurred. I got the unpleasant feeling of vertigo so I closed my eyes and tried to settle my internal gyroscope. My ears felt like I was underwater, so I swallowed and they popped. I opened my eyes and we were in darkness.

"Good luck," I heard Yorben say from my right. A small light appeared in his hand. It was a pebble, giving off a strong white light, allowing us to see the room. He held his hand out, offering Sir Locke the small stone.

"I be here if need me," Yorben said. I looked behind me and there was a set of blankets on the floor. It felt much like the Library basement room we had been in, but no candle and no books or parchment. Also, this room felt damp.

"Are we in Grimstone?" I asked.

"Let us find out," Locke said, getting to his feet. He wobbled a little, almost falling over. I too had trouble getting my balance and we ended up holding each other up like two sodden gnomes after the bar closes. When we got our 'land legs' back, we headed toward the stairs.

Unlike the Library room, there was no door, just the set of stairs going up. Locke held the stone out in front of him. Gnomes have excellent sight in the dark but it didn't hurt to have a light, especially if you are in strange surroundings.

When we exited the door at the top of the stairs, we found ourselves, not surprisingly, in another library. This was The Citadel, the largest library in all of Aethrofell, deep in the center of the capitol, Grimstone. Yorben had done us well.

Being a very large building, it took us a while to find our way out. And when we did, we found the city in upheaval.

We approached the large ornate doors at the entrance. The doors were actually too heavy for Sir Locke or I to open. It was good that they had guards at the doors that open them for visitors. We had to wait for one to allow us to exit.

The difference was shocking. It was like stepping through a portal in time. Within the walls of the library, everything was quiet, serene and peaceful. But just outside those doors, the city was the total opposite.

From our last visit to Grimstone, I knew the city was a fast-paced, bustling metropolis. There were dozens of three-story buildings and the Imperial Palace actually had five stories, with towers which could be seen from almost any place in Grimstone.

But this was not the normal bustle of city life.

No, this was near chaos.

Military cohorts were marching to and fro. Civilians were running with children or loaves of bread under their arms. Town criers were on every corner announcing a military lockdown of the city. All of the gates were being closed, battlements were being manned, and the elite Dragonborn 1st and 2nd divisions were being activated.

The Horde from the Great Grass Sea was approaching the city in full force.

Up until that day, the Horde was merely a nuisance to the Empire. They mostly waylaid caravans and unlucky travelers who strayed too far from the main Imperial roads, trying to benefit from a short cut through unpatrolled roads. Occasionally a band of the Horde, made up of the most despicable characters, would attack a small town. They would lay claim to the town, do bad things to good people until the local garrison sent out a squad of Imperial soldiers to put things right. Usually, these ill-fated raids ended with a lot of dead Horde and a few injured and scared townsfolk.

Orcs, goblins, and kobolds usually made up their number, nothing an Imperial squad couldn't handle. But from what I could make out from the town criers' announcements was that these cads had joined forces with the disgraced Dark Elves and a sect of Hill Giants. The elves were as clever and devious as the giants were stupid and strong. There also seemed to be a few other factions that had joined their ranks. All were in route to attack the Emperor's seat of power head on.

"They can't hope to succeed, can they?" I asked as I did my best to keep up with my friend.

"Obviously they do!" Locke shouted over his shoulder to me. It was hard to keep up and it was harder to communicate with all that was going on around us. We weren't the smallest people trying to get somewhere, but it was close.

There were children smaller, running around with wooden swords, making believe they were elite Dragonborn battling the Horde. There were other children in a chain, the youngest holding their older sibling's hand, who in turn held the next eldest's hand, and so on until the eldest held their mother's hand who held her husband's hand. All carrying as much food as they could. All rushing to one of the shelters. They reminded me of ducklings.

There were merchants rushing to get their goods back to their shops and homes. Military units marching from one post to another, cavalry heading toward the gates, and all manner of people going in all different directions.

And of course, there was us. I was doing my best to follow my friend whom I hoped knew where he was going.

"But how can they hope to win? The Emperor's Dragonborn haven't lost a serious battle in the Emperor's lifetime!" And the Emperor was over 500 years old by all accepted accounts. A feat unparalleled in human history. Humans just don't live that long. Even elves don't. I wondered if that was a mystery even my good friend couldn't solve.

"They don't need to win to succeed," was the shouted reply from ahead of me.

I doubled my efforts to catch up to Sir Locke. What he said had bothered me. But the way he said it, the desperation and sorrow in his voice, scared me more than I had ever been scared.

I fought through a crowd of tourists and looked around. I had lost him. He had been only a few yards ahead of me, but I lost him. I turned around in a circle trying to spot him. This was not the best use of my time since I knew he wasn't behind me. But I was starting to feel the panic that was permeating the crowds. He had to be somewhere ahead to the left, the right or straight ahead.

"Latswin!" The sharp tone cut through the cacophony around me.

"Locke?"

I looked around but couldn't see my friend.

"Up here"

I looked up and to my right to see my friend on the back of a horse.

"Locke?" I had no idea my friend knew anything about riding a horse.

He reached out his hand and I took it. With both hands, and surprising strength, he pulled my considerable girth up behind him, onto the horse's wide backside.

"You know how to ride a horse?"

"No, not in the least. But this isn't a horse, and I'm not leading him."

I looked past my friend and noticed for the first time that the horse's neck wasn't a neck at all but the torso of a man. The centaur turned back to me and said dryly, "neigh."

I sat in shocked silence.

My friend laughed.

"No time for comedy, we need to get to the palace without delay," Locke said in an admonishing tone that he failed to pull off. Probably because he couldn't stop laughing at my shock.

Luckily my reflexes were good because Locke's friend took off without further ado at full speed. I was just able to grab onto my friend's cloak or I would have rolled off the back of the centaur's rump. My friend also had to react quickly. He grabbed hold of the centaurs long braided hair and we were off.

"His name is Stanley, I met him on my last trip here," Locke explained.

"He speaks common?"

"He speaks six languages, is a decent thespian, and will talk your ears off if you let him."

We wove our way through crowds with amazing speed and agility. I was impressed.

"Why did you say they had already succeeded? Is their goal to lose?" I was very confused.

"Their goal is what you see all around you. They don't need to win the battle; they aim to win the war."

"You're not making a lot of sense." I usually had trouble keeping up with my friend's thought processes and this time was no different.

"Have you ever heard, 'the threat cuts as deep as the sword?'"

"No, what does that mean?" I asked.

"They want chaos. They want to create fear," Sir Locke explained.

"Why?"

"Because when people are afraid, they do not act rationally. They do not think. Instinct kicks in and they react too quickly, haphazardly, predictably."

"But the Emperor assuredly won't, he's been through this type of threat hundreds of times in his lifetime," I argued.

"But how long since it happened without all of his Aether Stones in place?"

"But they recovered it, and it's on its way back," I said.

"Yes. And likely already here."

"But how? It would take nearly a week riding full speed, without a stop, to reach Grimstone from Little Thoracia," I argued.

"How long did it take us?"

As was his way, Sir Locke forced me to think it through.

"So, you believe they teleported to the cohort and picked up the stone and teleported back?"

"I think so. They weren't in a rush to get it back, not enough of a rush to have wizards strategically stationed to bring it back. No, they didn't think there was an urgent need to get it back right away."

"But now there is. There's a full out attack," I said.

"At least that's the threat."

"The Horde must have found out the stone was stolen and figured it was a once-in-a-lifetime opportunity to attack the Emperor." I said, happy with my deductions.

"They knew the stone was stolen, because the minds behind this attack are also the ones who orchestrated the theft," Sir Locke declared.

"So that was their plan? To weaken the Emperor's defenses by stealing the stone and then attacking?"

"No. That would be doomed to failure. Even if the Emperor was missing the stone, they couldn't hope to win."

And my happiness with my reasoning faded away.

"I'm confused again," I confessed.

"I know. But I can't even tease you about it. I was duped also. This plan was years in the making and more than one genius criminal mind hatched it. This is a concerted effort. We're not up against one demented professor. There's a cabal, a sect."

"A conspiracy?" I asked.

"Of the highest order."

"But I still don't understand. We recovered the stone, and you believe it's already back in the emperor's hands, right?" I asked.

"Or it will be delivered just in the nick of time. A convenience that was the last clue," Locke said.

I could see the palace ahead. We were just a few minutes from the outer gates.

"Good timing?"

"Too good. And too convenient. A day earlier or a day later and their plan would have failed."

"What plan?" I asked.

"A plan to assassinate the Dragon Emperor by his own hand."

We didn't dismount when we reached the gates.

There was a full cohort guarding the main entrance, the gates were shut and barred.

No chance of entry there.

"There's no way you will gain an audience with all of this going on," Stanley said over his shoulder.

I could see my friend thinking. I know that sounds ludicrous, but I had come to know him better than I knew myself. He glanced up, toward one of the towers. There were guards there also. He looked at the gates again. He looked down one long expanse of wall, and then in the other direction, an equally long expanse of wall.

"There's nothing for it, we're beaten," Stanley said.

"Shhh!" Sir Locke hissed. I couldn't remember him ever being short with a friend, or actually even an enemy. Stanley didn't seem to notice or perhaps he didn't mind.

Locke pulled vial after vial out of his pockets. One held a blue liquid. Another green. Two purple. Another clear and one a deep blue so deep it was almost black.

"Can you throw us over that wall into the pile of hay within the gates?" Locke asked.

"What?" I asked.

"Sure…but they'll see you," Stanley answered.

"No, they won't," Locke said and whispered the simple plan so that we could both hear. I wasn't at all keen on the idea, but I admitted I could see no other way.

Our chauffeur, as he was, went back down the street we had come from until we were out of sight of the palace. Locke handed me one of the purple vials and unstopped one for himself. He tapped my vial genially, as if they were tankards of mead.

They most definitely were not.

"Bottoms up," he said as he downed his vial.

I followed suit.

"Is something supposed to happen?" I asked.

"Patience is more than a virtue, Latswin. It's a necessity for any good cleric. It is time you started practicing it."

In the middle of his lecture, my good friend, Sir Locke the gnome, disappeared before my eyes. It was as if he winked out of existence. Except I heard the rest of his admonishments coming from the same place, in the middle of Stanley's back.

"What now…" before I could finish I noticed that I too had vanished.

"Let's go, there's not a moment to waste," Locke whispered to Stanley.

Stanley galloped this time, and we had no easy time of staying on his back. He went straight toward the gate at what I thought must be full speed (Later Locke assured me I was wrong…it was nowhere near his full speed).

As expected, the Dragonborn Cohort took a defensive posture. The front row of soldiers went down on one knee and brought up their spears. The second row pulled back their bows, arrows notched and at the ready.

"Whoa now!" Stanley shouted. He stomped down hard with his front hooves to come to a jarring halt, but we never felt it because he used his forward momentum to buck his hind quarters straight into the air.

"Whoa whoa!" Stanley continued. We were easily tossed over the gate and the armed cohort guarding it. True to Stanley's word, we landed safely on the pile of hay. Two horses lunching at the pile neighed softly at the unexplained jostling of their stash.

I wondered how Stanley would explain his antics. "Sorry fellas. I heard there was an imminent attack and I rushed over here to volunteer my services in the defense of Aethrofell!" Stanley yelled. He put the town criers to shame. The extra noise he produced wasn't necessary as gnomes are stealthy by nature. We rarely make a sound when we don't want to.

"Let's be off Latswin, I fear we are already too late," Locke whispered right beside me.

I wondered if my friend could see me.

I couldn't see him, nor my own limbs, hands or feet.

I felt his hand take hold of my wrist and he started leading me toward the main doors of the palace.

It was then I realized why Stanley was still making such a racket. It wasn't to hide our passing, it was to bring someone, anyone, out of the palace proper.

As we neared the entrance, the doors swung open and five more Dragonborn came out and headed toward the commotion. I gasped at the sight of the Emperor's Elite Guard. They were magnificent.

They were dressed in much finer garb than the ones outside the gate. These had refined armor, white and blue braided ropes on their left shoulders, and crisp uniforms. They didn't carry spears or bows, only rapiers on their hips.

Locke tugged on my wrist, almost making me trip on the stairs. He hurried me through the open doors and into the vast receiving hall.

"Where to now?" I whispered. The receiving room was enormous. There were two different staircases winding upward, countless doors and open doorways to the left and right. And another massive set of double doors straight ahead.

"Follow me," Locke said. This time I aimed to hold onto *his* wrist. As he seemed to have no trouble finding me, while I had no idea where he was. I reached quickly for his withdrawing hand, but missed. Luckily, I caught the end of his cape which was already billowing out from his hurrying toward the double doors.

I had thought them closed, but they were slightly ajar. The guards on either side of the doors didn't notice as we slipped through the space that was too small for Dragonborn or humans.

Once inside this next room (as massive as the entry hall), Sir Locke hesitated for a moment and then took off again toward a door on our left.

Still hanging on to his cloak, I was able to follow along, albeit at a pace that was soon to leave me breathless.

This entryway also had guards, but luckily no door. It was just an open archway that led down a long corridor.

Once we were well past the guards, I whispered, "how do you know where to go?"

"These were the only paths with guards," he whispered back.

The hallway opened onto a T and we had to choose between right or left. I heard voices from the left.

"I think it's to the left," I whispered.

"Why?" was the simple answer.

"I hear voices," I said, a bit proud of myself.

"Then it must be this way," Locke said, pulling me down the corridor on our right, away from the voices.

"This is serious business, Latswin, soldiers won't be chit chatting if they are guarding the Emperor's path."

"You are really a genius, Locke," I said, amazed once again.

"Not really my friend, I came this way when I followed Dupreau." I could hear his smile although I couldn't see it.

After a slight turn to the right again, we found two stoic guards standing by a closed door.

Sir Locke stopped so abruptly that I bumped into him. This caused me to let out a soft gasp.

Dragonborn's ears must be very sharp because both guards turned toward us. I almost ran but then I realized we were still invisible.

We proceeded as stealthily as a Sprite walking on air. When we were a few yards from the guards, I heard Sir Locke whispering so softly, at first, I thought it was a draft of wind.

Then I heard a loud voice, which sounded just like Locke's, coming from the turn in the hall we had been at.

"No! I will not. The Emperor must never know!"

The guards didn't hesitate. They drew their swords and rushed past us to the bend in the hall.

The door opened a small amount (I presumed it was Sir Locke's doing) and still holding onto his cloak, I followed him through. I could tell he turned and closed the door quietly behind us.

"How did…" I began.

"A minor illusion. An elementary spell actually. They call it 'Throwing Your Voice.'"

This inner corridor was very well lit. There were twice as many torches as there were anywhere else we'd seen.

After 20 feet, the slope of the floor changed drastically and we found ourselves on a winding staircase hewn from stone. It went down into the depths below the palace.

When we reached the bottom, we traversed another hall and found another door. This time no guards.

The door opened with a little effort, and thankfully no sound. Slipping inside I saw an amazing sight. There were soldiers inside the doorway, Imperial Bodyguards. They should have heard us or seen the door open and close, but they were focused on what was happening on the raised dais ahead of us. They had taken two instinctive steps forward when they realized their emperor was in mortal danger.

We were too late.

The room was the smallest we'd seen so far. It was a circular room, with a 15-foot radius. There were no other doors. There were no torches along the walls, but instead very large clear gemstones that pulsed with light. They made the room seem like it was outside in broad daylight. Encircling the round dais were figures, all in the same blue and green robes, but of all different sizes, genders, and races. There was a Dragonborn, an Elf, a Dwarf, three Humans, an Aasmir, a Kenku, two Tieflings and a Halfling. They were all chanting, oblivious to what was happening on the dais.

On the raised platform in the middle of the room stood the Dragon Emperor himself. A tall Human, wearing shining armor, a sheathed sword the only adornment on him.

His hands were aloft, held up above his head. It looked as if he had just finished an incantation.

Around him, floating in the air were five glowing orbs, Aether Stones. Each was a different color. There was a very deep blue one, a fire-like red one, a white one with swirls of light blue and gray in it, a black one that seemed to pull in the light around it, and a green one.

And they weren't just floating. They were circling around the Emperor. Slowly, but definitely moving.

So why were the guards on high alert?

I looked closer and I could see the emperor's face. It showed shock and pain. He wasn't moving. He wasn't speaking. His mouth was open as if in mid-sentence, but nothing came out.

The guards looked at each other then back at the Emperor.

"Get him out of there!" Locke yelled.

They either thought the other yelled it or they were in too much shock to question where the voice came from.

Sir Locke's shout broke their paralysis and they leapt forward simultaneously. One was a little quicker than the other. He ducked beneath the circling orbs, and stepped onto the dais. He too seemed to freeze in place. The second, showing no regard for her personal safety did what her compatriot did, with equally dismal results.

Then I felt the cloak in my hand pull away.

"No!" I yelled.

But I didn't need to fear.

Locke wasn't going to add a fourth to those frozen in the circle. I saw his cloak blink into existence as he expertly tossed it up and over the deep blue orb. The one that had been stolen.

When the orb was covered three things happened in such a quick succession that I could not tell when one started and the previous ended.

First, all of the chanting stopped and the robbed mystics around the outside of the circle all fell to the ground.

Second, the three in the circle were freed of their paralysis and continued on with their previous movements. The Emperor gave out a moan of anguish and began falling to the floor. The fastest bodyguard reached the Emperor before he collapsed and caught him. The second bodyguard tripped over the lip of the dais and effectively tackled the first guard and the Emperor. All three ended up in a heap on the other side of the platform.

And the orbs stopped moving.

Being a cleric, albeit not a graduated one, I did what I was trained to do. I ran to the Emperor and checked for signs of life.   Luckily the two guards were still in somewhat of a state of shock, so they didn't notice me although I brushed against both of them at least once.

There was nothing I could do. The Emperor was under a powerful spell and the best I could tell, he was dying.

"What can you do?" Sir Locke whispered close to me.

The guards weren't just in shock, they were disoriented from the few moments under whatever spell had taken control of the Emperor.

"Nothing.   He needs an experienced cleric, and maybe they won't be able to help either."

I didn't think any of the robed characters lying unconscious around the outside of the room were clerics. They were likely all wizards.

"Get the Emperor to a cleric immediately!" Sir Locke said in a very commanding voice. His voice had a strange tenor to it. I had never heard him sound that way. I wondered if it was something else he had learned while away.

The guards didn't question where the voice came from, or the instructions. The female guard picked up the Emperor and put his mostly lifeless body over her shoulder. They rushed, as best they could, out of the room, without another word.

"What happened?" I asked Sir Locke.

"Perhaps we can find out," came back Sir Locke's voice. It came from the dais. I could see his cloak, still floating in the air with the orb beneath it, slowly lowering toward the floor. Then the cloak wrapped more fully around the orb, and then it disappeared.

"Let's go. I don't know how much longer we will remain invisible. I wasn't able to fully test this potion."

"Where is the stone?"

"I have it here, under my cloak."

I headed toward the sound of his voice and then I saw the door open again. I hurried to the door and was able to once again find a bit of my friend's cloak flowing behind him. I grabbed on tight. I didn't want to be alone in this place.

Halfway back to the library, we winked back into sight. It would have scared more than a few on the street, but with the chaos growing worse, no one paid us the slightest attention.

After working our way halfway through the crowds, I found myself wishing that Stanley were with us. I hoped he hadn't gotten arrested, or worse.

We finally reached the library and made our way to the basement room. Yorben, true to his word, was laying on his mats, napping.

Locke shook the wizard and he woke up with a "hmpf."

"What's this?" Yorben asked when Locke handed him the orb.

"An Aether Stone."

"Hmm." Yorben was even shorter on words than Locke.

"I'd like you to figure out how it was used to kill the Dragon Emperor," Locke said.

To this Yorben raised his right eyebrow.

He turned the orb in his hands. It was dark blue, but in the darkness of the basement room, I could see little sparks of electricity inside. Like a tiny lightning storm. And the blue swirled like storm clouds.

"Can I keep it?" Yorben asked with a hint of excitement.

"I'd say you'll have more than enough time with it. I fear the Emperor will not recover and the city will be in chaos for a long time. But when they do realize it is gone, someone will come looking for it," Locke said.

"Uh huh."

"How long will it take you?" Locke asked.

"*If* I can do it…I don't know."

"Are we staying here?" I asked.

"No. Our only lead was last seen in Little Thoracia and there's nothing we can do here. I heard that Airity was locked up in the dungeons, but I doubt they'll get anything out of him. And that's only if they figure out that he should be interrogated."

"Can't you consult with them?" I asked.

"With who? If the Emperor dies, or if he is out of commission, the city will likely be in chaos. Actually, the whole country might be in turmoil. When a dictator falls, no matter how benevolent, there will be a lot of fighting to find his replacement."

"And there's the invasion also," I said.

"I don't think that was a real threat, but you may be right, in the end. Factions that were held at bay for the last 500 years may try to take over," Locke said.

Yorben ignored us. He was fascinated with the Aether Stone.

"So, this lead?" I asked.

"René Dupreau. I'm sure Airity didn't tell her anything more than she needed to know, but she may have heard or seen something without realizing its importance."

"Or she may be part of the sect that pulled this off?" I asked.

Locke seemed to think this over.

"Or she could have been the mastermind, and Airity was her patsy," I offered.

"I don't think so. I think she was a hired hand, nothing more," Locke said with more hope than conviction.

"I guess we'll have to wait and see," I said.

My friend thought this over. He turned to me and put his hands on my shoulders.

"Sometimes that's all we can do, Latswin."

The End

Latswin

Want more?

You can find the first five books in the Sir Locke the Gnome series as ebooks on Amazon.

> A Case of Cranks and Pranks
> The Death of a Champion
> The Case of the Missing Crown
> The Case of the Restless Spirit
> The Case of the False Detective

Coming soon:
Audio books of the first five Sir Locke the Gnome books, read by Robert Feifar

Check out Martin's first novel, The Time Warp King, written with Alyssa Bishop. Available in paperback and ebook.

Like the cover art? Find more art by Joshua Duncan. On Twitter at @josh_cartoonguy or on Facebook at "Josh The Cartoon Guy"

Made in the USA
Monee, IL
25 November 2022